Magic Bullets

"Okay," Dover said, "the talking is over. Where's the money?"

"You're right," the man said, "the talking is over. I'm not giving you my money."

"Mister," Dover said, "you're lookin' down the barrels of three guns."

"If you fellas don't turn around and walk away now, I'll kill you."

They all laughed, and Dover asked, "How are you gonna do that?"

The man smiled and said, "Magic."

"Ain't no magic," Bennett said. "It's all tricks."

"Then I'll kill you," the man said, "with a trick."

"Boys," Dover said, cocking the hammer on his gun.

The others did the same . . .

Clint could see the men were cocking the hammers on their guns. He was pretty far away, so he drew his rifle from its scabbard and prepared to fire.

He was stunned by what happened next.

The man on the ground—previously unarmed—suddenly had a gun in each hand, and was firing. The three armed men were shot right off their saddles, dead before they hit the ground.

THE GUNSMITH

388

MAGIC MAN

J. R. ROBERTS

JOVE BOOKS, NEW YORK

THE BERKLEY PUBLISHING GROUP
Published by the Penguin Group
Penguin Group (USA) LLC
375 Hudson Street, New York, New York 10014

USA • Canada • UK • Ireland • Australia • New Zealand • India • South Africa • China

penguin.com.

A Penguin Random House Company

MAGIC MAN

A Jove Book / published by arrangement with the author

JOVE® is a registered trademark of Penguin Group (USA) LLC.
The "J" design is a trademark of Penguin Group (USA) LLC.

For information, address: The Berkley Publishing Group,
a division of Penguin Group (USA) LLC,
375 Hudson Street, New York, New York 10014.

ISBN: 978-0-515-15445-0

PUBLISHING HISTORY
Jove mass-market edition / April 2014

PRINTED IN THE UNITED STATES OF AMERICA

10 9 8 7 6 5 4 3 2 1

Cover illustration by Sergio Giovine.

ONE

On the side of the wagon were the words MAGIC MAN. The wagon was being pulled by a single horse, and there was one man in the seat, driving.

The wagon had just left the town of Sparks, Wyoming, where it had drawn quite a crowd in the street for a show. That was the reason the three men had followed it out of town.

Tom Dover was the leader of the three, who were—for the most part—petty thieves. They had never pulled a big job—like a bank, or a train—in their lives. Dover was in his early thirties, while Stu Bennett and Hal Smith were in their late twenties. They were all looking for a way to raise the level of their jobs. However, none of them had even the slightest ability to think big. Small time was all they would ever be.

"How much money you think he made in town, Tom?" Smith asked.

"I dunno," Dover said, "but you saw the crowd he drew."

"Gotta be a lot," Stu Bennett said. "Maybe hundreds!"

"Where do we take him?" Smith asked.

"About two miles up ahead there's a sharp turn in the road," Dover said. "Let's ride up ahead and wait for him there."

They each gave their horses a kick, gave the wagon a wide berth so they could ride on ahead of him and wait.

Clint topped a rise with Eclipse, his Darley Arabian, and stopped just to take a look around him. It was a beautiful fall day, the air smelled great, and it was quiet. So quiet, in fact, that he could hear the sound of a wagon below him. It creaked and squeaked on its axles. He stood in his stirrups and spotted it on the road below him, a Conestoga wagon with wooden sides, being pulled by a tired-looking horse.

Then he spotted something to his right, saw three riders ahead of the wagon on the road. They stopped and seemed to be waiting for the wagon at a sharp turn.

If it had been a stagecoach, he would have thought they were robbing it.

He watched with interest . . .

Tom Dover heard the wagon coming around the corner, told Bennett and Smith, "Get off the road. Let's not show our hand too early."

"Right." The two men rode their horses off the road behind some rocks.

The three of them waited.

Clint saw two of the men ride off the road and go into hiding. They were either planning to rob the wagon, or worse, and the man on the wagon was riding into it blindly.

"Come on, big guy," he said. "We're going to poke our noses in where they don't belong again."

* * *

As the wagon came around the turn, Tom Dover was sitting his horse, right in the middle of the road. The wagon driver reined in his horse and stared.

"Howdy, friend," he said.

"Howdy," Dover said. "Say, ain't you that Magic Man fella did a show in town?"

"That's me," the man said. "Did you see the show?"

"I did," Dover said. "It was really good."

"Thanks."

"How do you do all those magic things?"

"I can't tell you that, friend," the man said. "It's magic."

"Well, I got some magic of my own," Dover said.

"Is that right?" the man on the wagon said. "I'd like to see that."

"Watch," Dover said, "as I suddenly, magically, become . . . three men."

On cue, the other two men came riding out and stood one on each side of Dover.

"There you go," Dover said.

"I think your trick needs work," the Magic Man said.

"Is that right?" Dover asked. "Well, let's try this. Why don't you step down off that wagon right now."

"Why?"

"We're gonna do another trick," Dover said. "We're gonna make all your money disappear."

"I don't think you want to do that," the man said.

"I think we do," Dover said. He drew his gun. "Down!"

The other two men drew their guns, and the man on the wagon didn't have a choice.

TWO

The man stepped down from the wagon.

"Hold that coat open," Dover said.

The man did, holding the coat by the bottom and spreading it.

"He ain't armed," Bennett said.

"That's fine," Dover said. "That's the way we want him."

"So what do we do now, boys?" the man asked. He was tall, wearing a black coat and black pants, a derby hat, and a wrinkled white shirt. Like Dover, he looked to be in his thirties.

"Where's the money?" Dover asked.

"What money?"

"The money you collected for your show in town," Dover said. "Don't play stupid with us, Magic Man."

"Those are the proceeds of my show," the man said. "If I give you that, I'll be broke."

"That's okay," Dover said. "See, if you give it to us, we'll leave you alive and you can earn more money at the next town. If you don't give it to us, we'll kill you, and tear your wagon apart. We'll find it, and take it anyway."

"Doesn't sound like you're giving me much of a choice."

"No choice at all."

Clint knew he was taking too long to find his way down to the road. When he finally did reach it, he saw that the three mounted men had their guns out, and had forced the man on the wagon to step down. He was facing them, obviously unarmed.

Or so Clint thought . . .

"Okay," Dover said, "the talking is over. Where's the money?"

"You're right," the man said, "The talking is over. I'm not giving you my money."

"Mister," Dover said, "you're lookin' down the barrels of three guns."

"If you fellas don't turn around and walk away now, I'll kill you."

They all laughed, and Dover asked, "How are you gonna do that?"

The man smiled and said, "Magic."

"Ain't no magic," Bennett said. "It's all tricks."

"Then I'll kill you," the man said, "with a trick."

"Boys," Dover said, cocking the hammer on his gun.

The others did the same . . .

Clint could see the men were cocking the hammers on their guns. He was pretty far away, so he drew his rifle from its scabbard and prepared to fire.

He was stunned by what happened next.

The man on the ground—previously unarmed—suddenly had a gun in each hand, and was firing. The three armed men were shot right off their saddles, dead before they hit the ground.

Clint kicked Eclipse into a gallop, and as he rode up on the action, the man on the ground turned to face him.

Empty-handed.

"Take it easy," he said. "I'm here to help. At least, I thought you needed help."

"As you can see," the man said. "I'm fine."

Clint looked at the writing on the side of the wagon. It said, MAGIC MAN, in large print, and beneath that, it said, *Feats of Prestidigitation*.

"It sure looked to me like they had the drop on you," Clint said.

"Actually," the man said, "I had the drop on them."

"You mind if I check to make sure they're dead?"

"They're dead," the man said, "but go ahead and check."

Clint nodded, dismounted, and walked to the three bodies. They were, indeed, dead. Each had been hit several times, and they all looked like killing shots.

"Any one of these shots would've killed them," he said, turning to the man.

"I had to make sure," he said. "I couldn't take a chance. They were intending to rob and kill me."

"I saw that, from the ridge," Clint said, pointing. "I just couldn't get down here fast enough. I probably should have taken a shot from up there."

"That's okay," the man said. "I appreciate the thought."

"Well," Clint said, "I guess we better get them off the road."

"Let's put them in the back of my wagon," the man said.

"Why?"

"I'm going to take them to the next town and talk to the law," he said. "I don't need anybody to come looking for me."

"I get it."

"I could use you as a witness, if you don't mind," the man said. "Are you heading anywhere in particular?"

"No," Clint said, "just drifting. I'd be happy to come with you."

"Great," the man said. "Let's get them loaded."

Taking some blankets from the wagon, they wrapped each body, then lifted them up and loaded them into the rear of the wagon.

"By the way," Clint said when they were done, "my name's Clint Adams."

They shook hands, but the man didn't offer his name.

"What's your name?"

"Well," the man said, "as you can see on the wagon, I'm the Magic Man."

"Yes, but . . . that's not your name, is it?"

"No," the man said. "I'll tell you what, you can call me . . . Emrys." He pronounced it Em-er-rus.

"Emrys?"

"That's right."

"Okay, Emrys," Clint said, "let's get going."

THREE

Clint rode Eclipse alongside the Magic Man's wagon, and he and Emrys talked. It seemed to him that the man chattered incessantly, and yet by the time they reached the town of Ten Sleep, he realized he knew very little about the man.

Also, Emrys had not revealed whether or not he knew who Clint was.

As they entered Ten Sleep and drove down the main street, the Magic Man's wagon attracted a lot of attention.

"We better head right for the sheriff's office," Clint said. "Get those bodies out of your wagon."

"Suits me," Emrys said.

They found the office and stopped in front of it. Clint dismounted, and Emrys stepped down from his wagon. People began to crowd around it.

"You want to tell these people who you are and what you're about?" Clint asked. "While you've got them gathered?"

"Let's get the business at hand out of the way first," the magician said.

"Okay," Clint said, "let's go in."

They mounted the boardwalk and entered the sheriff's office.

A man was seated behind a desk, a pair of boots up on top. He was working on them with a cloth, trying to get a shine where there was no hope anymore. He was in his sixties, with tufts of white hair around a bald crown.

"Yeah?" he asked unpleasantly. "What can I do for you boys?"

"Sheriff," Emrys said, "I have three dead bodies in my wagon."

The sheriff reluctantly looked up from the gob of spit he had just deposited on one of his boots.

"What?"

"Dead men," Emrys said.

"Three of them," Clint added.

"In my wagon," Emrys went on, "out front."

"Dead men?" the sheriff repeated. "Who are they?"

"I don't know."

"How'd they die?"

"I killed them."

"Wha—why did you do that?"

"They were trying to rob me," Emrys said, "on the trail."

The sheriff finally decided he was finished with his boots. He took them off the desk, pulled them on while Clint and Emrys waited, and then stood up.

"Show me," he said.

"Just out here," Emrys said.

They all stepped outside to the wagon. Emrys opened the back so the sheriff could examine all three men. The crowd had not thinned, and now they "oohed" and "ahhhed" at the presence of the bodies.

"Know them?" Clint asked.

"I do," the sheriff said. "Three small-time would-be outlaws." He turned to Clint. "You help him kill 'em?"

"No, he did it all himself."

The sheriff examined the bodies again.

"They've been shot."

"That's right," Emrys said.

The sheriff studied him critically.

"You don't wear a gun?"

"I don't."

"What's your business, friend?"

"I do magic."

"Do what?"

"Magic," Emrys said. "I'm a magician." He reached into the sheriff's vest and brought out a bouquet of flowers. The crowd "ahhhed" again.

"What the—"

"Who wants these for his wife?" Emrys asked.

A man stepped forward and took them, showed them to his friends.

"Magic," he told the sheriff.

"Ain't no such thing."

"Is that right?" Emrys said. "I tell you what, Sheriff. Draw your gun and point it at me."

"What?"

"Go ahead, do it," Emrys said. "You won't hurt me."

"Mister, I don't take my gun out of its holster less'n I'm gonna use it."

"Don't worry, Sheriff," Emrys said, "you're not going to take it out now."

"Huh?"

"Go ahead, try it," the magician said.

The sheriff scowled, murmured, "Durned fool," and went

to draw his gun. He came out of his holster with a handful of flowers.

"Wha—" He threw the flowers down as if they were red hot. "Where's my damn gun?"

"Look in your holster."

The sheriff looked down, saw that his gun was still in his holster.

"How'd you do that?" he demanded.

Emrys smiled and said, "Magic."

FOUR

The sheriff grabbed some men from the crowd and had them carry the bodies over to the undertaker's office.

"I'll need you boys not to leave town," he told Clint and Emrys.

"I'll be at one of your hotels," Clint said. "Don't know which one yet."

"I guess I'll do the same, after I find someplace to put my wagon."

"Try Hanson's Livery," the sheriff said. "He's got enough room. End of the street."

"Thank you, Sheriff."

The sheriff set about dispersing the crowd, and then walked over to the undertaker's.

"I owe you a meal," Emrys said to Clint. "Let me get my wagon situated, and get myself a room, and I'll buy you a steak."

"Sounds good," Clint said. "We passed a hotel on the way in. I'll be there, if they have a room."

"Okay," Emrys said, "I'll meet you in the lobby."

They separated there, each going his own way for the time being.

In among the crowd were two men who recognized the dead men.

"That was Tom Dover and his boys," Ed Morley said. "Did you see?"

"I saw," Danny Roburt said.

"Whataya think the sheriff's gonna do about it?" Morley asked.

"The old man ain't gonna do nothin'," Roburt said.

"That's right," Morley said. "So we have to."

"Why?" Roburt said. "Those three were idiots."

"I know," Morley said, "but they were our friends."

"Your friends maybe."

"Look," Morley said as the sheriff shouted at the crowd to go home, "if they can be killed and nothin' gets done, it could happen to us. Somebody's got to pay for this."

"What the hell," Roburt said. "If I'm dead, what do I care if somebody pays for it or not? I'll be just as dead."

"Look, Roburt—"

"Forget it," Roburt said. "You wanna get revenge, get some of your other friends to do it with you. Not me. Not for those three."

As Roburt walked away, Morley thought he was right. He should talk to some of his other friends.

Emrys found Hanson's Livery and arranged for his horse and wagon to be stored.

"This is important," he said to Old Man Hanson. "Don't go in the wagon."

"I won't."

"I'm serious," he said. "There's magic in there that can kill you."

Hanson stared at the wagon.

"For real?"

"For real."

"Yer shittin' me!"

Emrys waved his hand and a puff of smoke appeared in the air between them. Hanson stepped back from it, his eyes going wide.

"Magic," the magician said.

Hanson watched as the smoke rose, and dissipated.

"Do not go in the wagon," Emrys said again.

"Yes, sir," Hanson said. "I mean, no, sir. I won't go in the wagon."

FIVE

Clint was waiting in the lobby when the magician showed up. He came down from the second floor, so Clint knew he was staying in the same hotel.

"Ready for that steak?" Emrys asked.

"I don't know," Clint said. "Is it going to be cooked, or are you going to make it appear from thin air? Or do you only do that with guns?"

"I don't know what you're talking about," Emrys said. "Let's go find a café that makes steaks."

"Suits me," Clint said.

They left the hotel and started walking down the street. As they passed people, they were stared at. Ten Sleep was a small town, and the word had already gotten around.

"Are they looking at me or you?" Emrys asked.

"I'm going to bet on you," Clint said.

"But you're the one who's famous."

"Not a lot of people know me on sight," Clint said. "But you rolled in today with that wagon, with three dead men in the back. And that hat . . ."

Emrys touched his derby and said, "What's wrong with my hat?"

"It's a little . . . different."

"And that's bad?" Emrys asked. "I thought this was what was worn in this time."

"Excuse me?"

"I mean, in the West."

"Well," I said, "it's real popular in the East, but not so much in the West."

Emrys frowned.

"How could my information have been so wrong?"

"I don't know," Clint said, even though it seemed the man was asking himself the question. "Here's a café, probably as good as any."

They crossed the street and went inside.

Morley saw the two strangers entered the café. He took up a position across the street, and watched while he tried to decide who he could bring in on this deal.

They sat at a back table and, under the watchful eye of the other diners, ordered steak dinners from the waiter.

"Can you make all these people disappear?" Clint asked.

"No, but maybe you can," Emrys said.

"I meant bloodlessly."

"Oh."

"Where are you from, Emrys?"

"Someplace far away," the magician said.

"In the East?"

"Farther."

"Europe?"

Emrys thought about that, then said, "Yes, Great Britain."

"How long have you been in this country?"

"Not long."

"You don't have much of an accent."

"I'm a fast learner."

"What are your intentions?"

"Just to travel around, entertaining people," Emrys said. "I have had vast responsibilities for a very long time. Now I just want to relax."

"And do magic tricks?"

"It is a way to make a living."

"Traveling is a good way to relax," Clint said. "I do it myself."

"Is that what you are doing now?" Emrys asked. "Traveling aimlessly?"

"That's it."

"So then you are in no hurry to leave?"

"This town?" Clint asked. "There doesn't seem to be much here."

"No, I mean leave me."

"Why? What did you have in mind?"

"I could use some company," Emrys said. "I have been talking to my horse for weeks. He doesn't answer."

Clint laughed.

"Also, I could use a guide. As you say, I have been traveling aimlessly. Perhaps, with your help, I can get to larger towns where I could make more money for my performances." Emrys hesitated, then added, "I could pay you."

Clint thought about the offer and said, "This is something we can keep talking about while we eat."

"Excellent," Emrys said.

They talked over two delicious steaks, continued over coffee and pie.

"You know," Clint said, "I can see my way clear to traveling with you for a while."

"That's wonderful," Emrys said.

"And you won't have to pay me," Clint said. "It'll be fun for me to watch you work."

"I won't be able to show you how any of my magic is done," Emrys warned.

"That's okay," Clint said. "It might even be more fun that way."

SIX

"Speaking of tricks . . ." Clint said before they left the café.

"What about them?"

"I saw those three laying in wait for you, and I couldn't get down there in time," Clint said. "I thought you were as good as dead—especially when I saw you on the ground, unarmed, and they had their guns out."

Emrys waited.

"Where did the guns come from?"

"What guns?"

"The guns you used to kill them."

Emrys finished the last bite of pie on his plate, pushed it away from him. He sat back in his chair and stared at Clint.

"We have already established that I will not be showing you how my tricks work."

"So it was a trick," Clint said. "Some kind of . . . what? Sleight of hand?"

"Magic," Emrys said.

"Real magic," Clint said.

Emrys shrugged.

"Is there any other kind?"

"Okay," Clint said, "so you're not going to tell me where the guns came from."

"No."

"Fair enough."

They settled their bill and walked outside. Clint stopped Emrys right there on the boardwalk, putting his hand on the other man's arm.

"What is it?" the magician asked.

"We're being watched."

"Yes," Emrys said, "by everyone."

"No, I mean specifically," Clint said. "He followed us to the café."

"One man?"

"Yes."

"You are the Gunsmith," Emrys said. "You don't worry about one man, do you?"

"I worry about everybody," Clint said. "That's how I've managed to stay alive this long."

"I thought perhaps," Emrys said, "it was magic."

"Right. Let's just be aware as we walk."

"And where are we walking to?"

"I thought we might have a drink," Clint said. "Then turn in and get an early start in the morning."

"To go where?"

"To your next show."

"And where will that be?"

"I don't know," Clint said. "I'll have to think about it and tell you in the morning."

"Then I think a drink sounds good."

They found the nearest saloon and, once again, attracted attention when they entered.

"The entire town must have seen us ride in," Emrys said as they moved to the bar.

"Or word has gotten around," Clint said. "Some of these men might have known the dead man. That might be why we're being followed."

"By a friend of theirs, you mean?"

"Yes."

"So someone will be looking for vengeance."

"Somebody usually is." Clint signaled to the bartender, who reluctantly came over. "Two beers."

The bartender's reluctance continued as he drew the beers and set them down in front of Clint and Emrys.

"Thanks," Clint said.

They both drank half their mugs down and set them on the bar.

"It's probably not a good idea for you to be walking around unarmed," Clint said.

"I do not carry guns."

"But you're so good with them."

"Not really."

"I saw you shoot, Emrys," Clint said. "You killed three men who already had their guns out. That's the stuff of legends in the West."

"Then you must keep what you saw to yourself," Emrys said. "I have no desire to be a legend."

"Well," Clint said, "I can't say I blame you for that."

"I have known men who were said to be legends," Emrys said. "It is a heavy title to carry. You know that better than most men."

"I do," Clint said. "Don't worry, I'll keep my mouth shut."

"Thank you."

At that moment the batwings opened and the sheriff walked in.

"However," Clint said, "I don't know if the sheriff will do the same."

Emrys turned and looked at the lawman, who saw them and started over.

"It looks like we are about to find out."

SEVEN

"Gents," the lawman said.

"Sheriff," Clint said.

Emrys simply nodded.

"Beer, Sheriff?" Clint asked.

"Don't mind if I do," the sheriff said.

"I don't think we caught your name, Sheriff," Clint said as he waved to the bartender.

"Carlyle," the lawman said, accepting a beer from the bartender with a nod. "Sheriff Don Carlyle."

"Well, Sheriff Carlyle," Clint said, "did you get the dead men situated?"

"They have no family around here," the lawman said. "They'll be buried on boot hill, no headstones, just a marker."

"It is all they deserve," Emrys said.

"I suppose you'd feel that way since they tried to rob you," Carlyle said. "I just think there should always be something to mark the fact that a man was here."

"A good man should be remembered," Emrys said.

"I'm wondering," the sheriff said to Emrys, "how you managed to kill three men who had the drop on you."

"It was either luck," Emrys said, "or magic."

The sheriff laughed.

"Magic?"

"Almost everything I do involves magic, Sheriff," Emrys said.

"Like putting flowers in my holster?" Carlyle said. "That was . . . trickery."

"Tricks, magic," Clint said. "Sounds like the same thing to me."

"Don't tell me a man like you believes in this magic nonsense?" the lawman asked.

"I don't know," Clint said. "I just like to keep an open mind."

"So do I," Carlyle said, "but not that open." He drank his beer down, set the empty mug on the bar. "I wanna warn you two. Those fellas did have some friends around town. I'd be careful."

"Appreciate the warning, Sheriff," Clint said, "but if there's one thing I always am, it's careful."

"Suit yourself."

"Besides," Clint said, "we'll be leaving town in the morning."

"That's good," the sheriff said. "I don't need no trouble here."

"I am not looking for trouble, Sheriff," Emrys said, "I assure you."

"Yeah, you wasn't lookin' for it out there either, and it found you," Carlyle said. "Just watch yourself while you're in my town."

Emrys said, "Thank you for the concern," but the sheriff was out the door before he could hear it.

Clint and Emrys looked at each other, then looked around

the saloon. They were still drawing stares from most of the customers, as well as the girls who were working the floor.

"Let's finish up our beers," Clint said.

Emrys nodded.

Harriet—who everyone called "Harry"—and Diane were two of the four girls working the floor of the crowded saloon.

"Which one do you want?" Diane asked.

"I want the cute one with the magic," Harry said. "I want him to do some magic on me."

"Good, 'cause I want the Gunsmith. I ain't never been with anybody like him before."

"What if they don't wanna be with us?" Harry asked.

"Two beautiful young gals like us?" Diane asked. "What kind of man would turn all this down?"

"How do we do it?" Harry asked.

"Just follow my lead."

Clint and Emrys were finishing their beers when the two girls sidled up alongside them.

"Hello," Diane said.

Emrys looked at both girls, said, "Hello, fair ladies."

"Girls," Clint said.

"You fellas plan on bein' in town long?" the blond Diane asked.

"Not long at all," Emrys said. "In fact, we will be leaving your fair town tomorrow."

" 'Fair town,' " brown-haired Harry said. "You're so cute."

"Well, thank you."

"It would be a shame for you fellas to spend your only night in town alone," Diane said.

"So I guess we'll just volunteer to keep you company," Harry said.

"That is very kind of you," Emrys said.

"I don't think we have the money—" Clint said, but Diane cut him off.

"We ain't lookin' for any money," she said, pressing her hip up against Clint's. "Just company."

"Where are you sayin', cutie?" Harry asked Emrys.

"We are at the hotel just down the street."

"Good," she said. "I'll see you later." She hip-bumped him and walked away.

"After work," Diane told them, and did the same to Clint before moving off.

"Lovely young women," Emrys said.

"Yes."

"Are they harlots?"

"Are they . . . what?"

"Harlots."

"No, I heard you," Clint said. "That's just not a word you hear around here often."

"What do you call them here?"

"Well, the kind of women you're talking about we call prostitutes, or whores."

Emrys made a face.

"Much too crude."

"Apparently those two are just saloon girls, and not . . . harlots."

"Well, that is good," Emrys said. "I like serving wenches—I mean, saloon girls."

"I think we need to go back to our rooms," Clint said. "Looks like we're going to have company, and I'd like to freshen up."

"A fine idea," Emrys said. "I, too, need to freshen myself."

They left the saloon and walked back to the hotel.

EIGHT

Ed Morley watched the front of the hotel, was about to go in when he saw the sheriff enter. After that, even after the lawman left, he remained in the shadows across the street.

When Clint Adams and the magician had left the saloon, he'd followed them as discreetly as he could back to their hotel. They went inside, apparently for the night. The fact that they had turned in early gave him plenty of time to round up some help.

Clint walked Emrys to his door and said, "Stay away from your window."

"You really think someone will try to kill me?"

"I don't know," Clint said, "but there's no point in making it easy for them."

"All right," Emrys said, "I will stay away from the window."

"I'll see you in the lobby in the morning," Clint said. "We can have breakfast first and then leave this town."

"All right."

"By morning I'll have some idea where we can go to get you a good audience."

"Good night, then."

Clint went into his own room and, despite what he had told Emrys, went right to the window. He saw the man in the shadows across the street, but also saw him walk away. There was no telling what he was planning, but Clint stuck the back of a chair beneath the doorknob anyway.

He removed his boots and hung his gun belt on the bedpost. Getting comfortable on the bed, he thought about his new friend, Emrys. To say the least, he was an odd man, with mannerisms and a way of speaking that were unusual in the West. And what he had done against the three would-be robbers was incredible. Clint still didn't know where the man had gotten the guns he'd used, but he'd wielded them with a deadly proficiency that was impressive.

He had agreed to travel with Emrys because the man needed a guide, and he really was just wandering these days. But he was also very curious about the man, and wanted to find out as much as he could about him.

He also wanted—if he could—to keep the magician alive and well.

In his room, Emrys got comfortable on the bed, staring at the ceiling. All he had with him in the room was an extra shirt. His bag of tricks was still in his wagon. He hoped that the hostler would not try to get into his wagon, because if he did, bad things would happen. There were certain safeguards he had put in place to assure the safety of his property, his tricks—and his life.

He was not happy that he'd had to kill the three men who had tried to rob him. Except for his magic, his intention in the West had been to keep a low profile, but he now saw how difficult that would be. He was happy, however, to have made the acquaintance of Clint Adams. As the Gunsmith, he knew all about attracting unwanted attention, and how to deal with it. He would now also be instrumental in helping Emrys finding the best venues for his performances, where he could make the most money.

And should anyone else try to rob him or, worse, kill him, he knew he would have the right man with him to watch his back.

Clint Adams was a warrior of the West, and sort of reminded Emrys of those warriors of old, the Knights of King Arthur's Round Table.

Ed Morley had a problem.

He could not find anyone who considered the three dead men friends.

In fact, he could not find anyone who considered him to be a friend.

He lingered at the bar in a small saloon, staring into his half-finished beer.

"What's the big deal, Morley?" the bartender asked.

"The deal is, we can't just let a stranger come here and kill three of us without making him pay."

"And you're gonna make him pay?" the bartender asked. "He's got the Gunsmith backin' his play."

"I know," Morley said angrily. "Why do you think I'm tryin' to find men to back my play?"

"Come on, Morley," the bartender said, "who you gonna find to go against the Gunsmith? And a magic man?"

"He ain't no magician," Morley said. "He's got cheap tricks."

"How do you know?" the bartender asked. "You seen him perform?"

"Ain't no such thing as magic," Morley said.

"Well," the bartender said, "it'll be magic if you find anybody to back you."

NINE

Most hotels in the West—hell, most hotels anywhere—had creaking floorboards in the hall. Those boards had saved Clint's life ten times over.

When he heard the boards this time, he figured it was the girl coming, but many times he'd been waiting for a woman only to face a gun. He grabbed his gun from his holster and padded in his stocking feet to the door. He was standing there when someone knocked.

"Who is it?"

"It's Diane," she said. "Who did you think it would be?"

He opened the door and looked out. She appeared to be alone. If someone had been standing to her right or left, out of sight, Clint would have felt it. After all these years, those kinds of things did not get by him.

He opened the door wide and she saw the gun.

"Whoa," she said. "You were expecting someone else, weren't you?"

"I'm always expecting someone else," he said, backing off. "Come on in."

He walked to the bedpost and holstered the gun. She closed the door behind her. She was still wearing her saloon dress, with a shawl over it.

"I guess you're a careful man," she said.

"That's what comes from having a reputation."

"Must be a hard way to live."

"You get used to it."

She looked around.

"Do you have anything to drink?"

"No, sorry," he said.

"That's all right," she said, dropping her shawl to the floor. "I didn't come here to drink, did I?" She reached behind her back, then shrugged, and the gown joined the shawl on the floor.

"No," he said, "you obviously didn't."

She had smooth, pale skin; small but hard, round breasts; and a pretty, light pubic patch. Her hands were behind her back, and her breasts were pushed out slightly.

"Am I what you expected?" she asked.

"More," he said. "Much more."

"Thank you, sir."

She walked toward him, brought her hands around from behind her back, and started to unbutton his shirt. He put his hands on her hips. The skin was hot to the touch. She smelled of the saloon, but beneath it was her own heady scent, which eventually took over.

She had her hands inside his shirt the first time they kissed . . .

Emrys was lying on his back on the bed, thinking of long-gone friends, when there was a knock on his door. He got off the bed, walked to the door, and opened it. Harriet stood in the hall, looking surprised.

"You open the door that fast, without asking who it is?" she asked.

"Why not?" he asked.

"Your friend Clint Adams would be more careful than that," she told him.

"He has to be," Emrys said. "Nobody here knows me."

"I've heard your name bein' said around town."

"Then perhaps you should come in and tell me about it," he said, standing back.

"Thank you for the invitation." She stepped into the room, and the magician closed the door.

"May I take your shawl?"

"Uh, sure."

He took it from her smooth shoulders and tossed it aside.

"Do you have anything to drink here?" she asked, looking around.

"I am sorry, no."

"That's okay."

"What have you heard about me?" he asked.

"I heard somebody in town is looking for some men to help him get revenge on you."

"Revenge?"

"For the men you killed."

"They had friends?"

"Well," she said, "apparently one. But it sounds like he's having some trouble finding help."

"That is probably not because of me."

"No, you're right," she said. "It's because of the Gunsmith."

"Won't you sit?" he asked.

"Thanks." She looked around, then sat on the bed. He sat next to her.

"Most men would have been all over me by now," she

said. "All hands and drool. You do know why I came up here, don't you?"

"I have an idea."

"Then why haven't you kissed me yet?"

"I am a gentleman."

"Really? I haven't met many of those. How does a gentleman make love?"

"With care."

She smiled.

"I haven't had much of that either," she said. "It sounds interesting. Do I have to be naked for that?"

"That is usually the custom."

She stood up in front of him, reached behind her, and dropped her dress to the floor. She was buxom, and her long brown hair almost covered her large nipples.

"Will this do?" she asked.

"That will do just fine," he said, reaching for her.

She came into his arms eagerly, pressing her warm flesh to his face. He kissed her belly, then lifted his head to do the same to her breasts. She cradled his head, pushing his face into her full breasts. He found the nipples and bit them hard, then licked them.

He slid his hands around to her back, then slid them down so he could rub her buttocks.

"The bed," she said in a breathy tone, "we need to lie on the bed."

"Do we?"

He looked up at her and she smiled.

"My legs are already weak," she told him.

TEN

Diane's body appeared to be very sensitive. Every time Clint touched her, she seemed to catch her breath, bite her lower lip.

As she stood in front of him, he reached around and cupped her buttocks in his hands. He ran one finger down the crack between her cheeks. That was the first time her breath caught. Then he pulled her to him, burying his face between her breasts. He kissed her sweet flesh, then moved to her nipples. When he took one between his teeth, her breath caught again, then she moaned. Later the two girls would compare notes about how similar their experiences were. Almost as if one of the men knew what the other was doing, and copied him.

Strange.

Clint bit and sucked her nipples while she moaned and writhed in his grip, then he stood, turned, and lay her on the bed. She smiled up at him.

"You don't waste time, do you?" she asked.

"With a woman like you," he said. "wasting time is a waste of time."

She frowned, misunderstanding him. "What do you mean, a woman like me?"

"Beautiful," he said, "sweet, sweet tasting, extremely sensitive."

"I am sensitive," she said. "You don't know how much. No man does, because I've never met a man who bothered to find out."

"So," he said, getting on the bed with her, "let's find out . . ."

In the other room, Harry soon tired of Emrys's gentlemanly ways.

"I think," she said after they'd kissed for a while, "you should start being a little less of a gentleman."

"It will be hard to go against my upbringing," he said, "but I will try."

She slid into his lap and put her arms around his neck. He buried his face in that neck and kissed her, moving his hands around. He cupped her breasts, used his thumbs on her nipples, and then slid one hand into her lap. When he touched her there, she grew wet.

"Wow," she said, "your hands really are magic, aren't they?"

"No magic here, Harriett," he said. "In this room with you, I am just a man."

"Well," she said, tightening her arms around his neck, "a man is just what I'm looking for."

He stood up, carrying her in his arms, turned, and put her on the bed.

"Finally," she said.

"Watch me," he said, "make my clothes disappear."

* * *

Clint settled down between Diane's thighs, used his mouth and tongue to get her good and wet—so wet it soaked into the sheet beneath her. She did more than catch her breath then. She moaned and groaned, sighed and screamed, albeit silently. She reached down and held his head in place while he continued to work her until she almost stopped breathing. She held it, her body growing taut like a bow, and then she was bucking wildly beneath him.

When she stopped bouncing on the mattress, he slid up to lie beside her, his hands still working her.

"God," she said, pushing his hands away, "I told you I was sensitive. Give me a minute."

"No good?" he asked.

"Too good," she said, "that's the problem. I need a minute."

He kissed her shoulder and said, "I can give you a minute—just about."

She rolled over to put her head on his shoulder.

"I hope Harry's having as much fun with your friend," she said.

"I don't know about that," Clint said. "He seems to be much more of a gentleman than I am."

"Oh," she said, "Harry will cure him of that. She's got the kind of body—well, I shouldn't sell her to you. You might leave me here and go and join them."

"Two reasons I wouldn't do that," he said.

"And what are they?"

"You have a pretty nice body yourself."

"And the other reason?"

"I don't like to share."

"Actually," she said, sliding her hand down between his legs, "neither do I."

"Hey," he said, "I thought you said you needed a minute."

"A minute's up," she said. She kissed his chest, his stomach, kissed all the way down to his hard cock, then kissed it for a while. Finally she cupped his balls in one hand, wrapped her other hand around the root of his cock, and took it into her mouth. She spent a lot of time sucking him, wetting him thoroughly, squeezing his cock and his balls at the same time, getting him all worked up until he couldn't hold back any longer. He exploded into her mouth. She moaned, kept him in her mouth until he was finished, then released him, sat back on her heels, wiped the corners of her mouth with her fingers, and said, "Now it's you who needs a minute."

"Or more," he said.

Harry rolled away from Emrys and tried to catch her breath.

"My God," she said, "that *was* magic."

"Well," he said, "maybe just a little."

She looked over at him. Was he even handsomer than she'd thought he was? It seemed as if her eyes wouldn't focus on him.

"Um, are you . . ."

"Am I what?" he asked.

"Are you . . . all right?"

"I am fine," he said, reaching out and touching her body, "but you need sleep."

"Mmm," she said, suddenly very, very drowsy, "I think you're right."

In moments she was asleep, snoring very gently and sweetly.

Emrys smiled.

ELEVEN

Clint was happy to find Emrys waiting for him in the lobby in the morning.

"I stayed away from the window, as you told me," Emrys said.

"Good," Clint said. "So did I. Let's have some breakfast."

They went into the hotel dining room and Clint ordered steak and eggs. They did not talk about the night they'd each spent with Diane and Harry.

"Is that a traditional Western breakfast?" Emrys asked.

"I don't know if it's traditional," Clint said, "but it's what I usually have."

Emrys looked at the waiter and said, "I will have the same thing."

"Yes, sir," the waiter said.

"And coffee," Clint said. "Black and strong."

"Comin' up, sir."

"Strong?" Emrys asked.

"Very strong."

"Is that traditional in the West?"

"Yes," Clint said, "trail coffee is traditionally very strong, but mine is even stronger."

"This will be very interesting," Emrys said.

The waiter brought a pot and two cups, poured them full. Clint tasted the coffee before Emrys.

"It's strong," he pronounced, "but mine is stronger."

Emrys tasted the coffee and his eyebrows went up.

"This is not as strong as yours?" he asked.

"No."

"Amazing."

"You'll get to taste it on the trail," Clint said, "which is something I want to talk to you about."

"I am ready."

"I just wonder how much you have in your wagon in the way of supplies," Clint said. "Would I be able to get a look inside?"

"No one has ever been in my wagon," Emrys said. "There is a lot in there that men should not see."

"Uh-huh," Clint said. "If we're going to be traveling together, we're each going to be seeing everything the other has to offer."

"I understand," Emrys said.

"So what's the verdict?"

The waiter came with their food at that moment, setting their plates in front of them.

"Let us enjoy our breakfast," Emrys said, "and then I will take you to see my wagon."

"Good," Clint said. "We might need to buy some supplies before we leave town."

They cut into their steaks and started eating.

Clint followed Emrys into the livery stable. The hostler looked surprised to see them, moved away from the horse he was shoeing.

"Help you, gents?" he asked. "Interested in your horses? They're doin' well—especially yours, Mr. Adams. That is one healthy animal."

"Thanks," Clint said, "but we're here to see my friend's wagon."

"Ah," the man said, "I have that in the back."

"Not outside, I hope," Emrys said.

"No, no," the man said, "my place is big enough. Come on."

They followed him to the back, which was another whole section of the stable. The wagon stood there, looking secure. The rear doors of the wagon not only closed, but locked.

Emrys approached the wagon, stood in front of the doors for a moment, then looked at the older man, the hostler.

"I didn't try to get in," the man said. "I swear."

"I know," Emrys said. "If you had, I would know."

"Thanks," Clint said. "We just need to take care of some business. You can go back to work."

"You gonna open it?" he asked.

"Yes," Emrys said.

"Can I look?"

"No," the magician said. "Take Mr. Adams's advice and go back to work."

"Okay, yeah, sure," the man said.

As he left, Clint asked, "How would you have known if he tried to get in?"

Emrys looked at him and said, "I would be able to feel it if he did."

"Really?"

"I have certain safeguards in place which must be removed before we can go in."

Clint felt like this was part of the show.

"All right," Clint said, "remove them."

Emrys stood in front of the doors, lowered his head, and pressed his hands together. Clint expected some kind of fireworks, but when Emrys raised his head, he said, "Very well. We can go in."

Emrys reached for the doors.

TWELVE

Clint looked into the wagon and what he saw was . . . darkness.

"Wait here," Emrys said.

He climbed into the back of the wagon, which barely moved beneath his weight. Clint heard him moving around inside. He didn't know why he got the feeling the wagon was larger on the inside than on the outside. For a moment he thought Emrys might have gotten lost inside, but then suddenly the magician struck a match and lit a lantern.

"All right," he said, "you can come in."

Clint climbed up into the rear of the wagon. He was impressed by how sturdy it felt beneath his feet.

He looked around. On one side was what looked like a small worktable. Underneath were some sacks, which he assumed held some supplies.

"This other side swings out," Emrys explained, "so I can use it as a stage."

"I see. What's in these sacks?"

"Various supplies, including some flour and coffee."

"Any beans or bacon?"

"No."

"Beef jerky?"

"No."

"Okay, we'll need some," I said. "Do you have any money?"

Emrys looked at Clint.

"That's what they were trying to steal from me," he said, "my money. So yes, I have some."

"I thought we'd split the cost of the supplies."

"That suits me."

Clint looked around.

"I have to say, I'm a little disappointed."

"Why?"

"I expected something . . . different."

"Different how?"

"Scarier."

"I don't scare people, Clint," Emrys said. "I do magic tricks."

"Right, right," Clint said. "My mistake. Why don't we go and buy those supplies, and then we can get on the trail."

"All right," Emrys said, "but I had better lock up again. I don't want to tempt the hostler."

They stepped out and Emrys closed the doors behind them.

"You didn't lock it," Clint said.

"It is locked."

"Without a key?"

"Trust me," the magician said. "It's locked."

Clint almost grabbed the doors and checked, but in the

end he decided to trust Emrys, and they walked out of the livery together.

In the general store, Emrys stood around looking at everything while Clint picked out their supplies. The magician showed some interest in a glass jar filled with licorice so Clint tossed some of that into the mix.

"Say," the clerk said, "is that that magic fella?"

"That's him."

"He really do magic?"

Clint decided to go along with Emrys's act.

"He sure can."

The man was older, and was probably also the owner of the place.

"Hey," he said, "make 'im do something magic, huh?"

"I can't make him do anything," Clint said, "but if you were to, say, offer him some free licorice, I'll bet he could . . . conjure up something."

We both looked at Emrys, who didn't seem to be listening to us.

"What do you say, Emrys?"

The magician looked at him.

"Something magic for licorice?"

Emrys walked over to the counter. He studied the clerk, who stood expectantly, then the magician reached out and seemed to take a dollar out of the man's ear.

"Hey," the man said, "how did you do that?"

"Like this," Emrys said. He reached out for the other ear, and seemed to remove a dollar in change, which he allowed to cascade to the countertop.

"Well, I'll be damned."

"How much for the supplies?" Clint asked. "Oh, uh, minus the two dollars, of course."

*   *   *

Once outside, they started their walk back to the livery, carrying their purchases.

"So how *did* you do that?" Clint asked.

"I cannot help it if the man carries money around in his ears."

"No," Clint said, "I mean it."

Emrys looked at Clint.

"You know," he said, "the longer we ride together, the more you will begin to believe in real magic."

Clint wondered if the man was right.

THIRTEEN

They stowed the new supplies in the back of the wagon. Emrys would not let Clint enter it, but he was able to reach in and hand the supplies to the magician.

"How do you have room for all the supplies, and all your tricks?" Clint asked when they were done.

"Perhaps," Emrys said, "the wagon is larger than it appears."

"More magic?"

Emrys shrugged.

"I think," Clint said, changing the subject, "the next thing we should do is buy you a new horse. The one you got looks pretty tuckered out."

"Well," Emrys said, "that animal has come a very, very long way."

"We can talk to the hostler here about buying a new horse," Clint said.

"As you say," Emrys said. "You are the expert here."

They looked at some horses the hostler had in a corral behind the stable and Clint picked one out, a sturdy-looking six-year-old mare who wouldn't have any trouble at all pulling Emrys's wagon.

They walked the new horse into the stable and hitched it to the wagon. Then Clint saddled Eclipse, and they walked the whole outfit outside to find the sheriff waiting for them with a relieved look on his face.

"Just thought I'd see you fellas off," he said.

"You mean you wanted to make sure we were really leaving," Clint said.

He grinned.

"That, too."

"Well, we're on our way, all right," Clint said. "Thanks for the hospitality."

"I believe we may have someone following us, though," Emrys told the sheriff.

"What makes you say that?"

"A lady told me there was a man interested in getting revenge for the three dead men."

"Well, those three didn't have many friends in town," the sheriff said.

"There must be one," Clint said. "He's been following us, watching us."

"I don't know who that would be," he said, "but I'll watch you fellas as you ride out of town, if you want. Keep you safe."

"Why, thanks," Clint said, "that makes me feel so much safer."

The sheriff ignored the sarcasm in Clint's voice.

Emrys climbed up into his seat, picked up his reins, and Clint mounted Eclipse.

"So long, Sheriff," Clint said. "I don't expect we'll ever see each other again."

"That suits me," the sheriff said.

"Actually," Clint said, "it suits me, too."

Emrys shook his reins at the new horse and they started off down the street.

Morley watched Clint Adams and the magician ride out of town. He did so from the window of his room, so there was no chance that Adams—or the sheriff—would spot him. When they were out of sight, he left his room and went downstairs. He left the building and ran to the livery stable to get his own horse.

As he saddled the animal, he asked the hostler, "Were you here when the magician left?"

"I was."

"Do you know where they're goin' next?"

"Nah, I didn't hear anything. Why?"

"I—I just liked his act. I wanna see it again."

"Well," the man said, "that wagon shouldn't be too hard to follow."

"Yeah," Morley said, mounting up. "Yeah."

The sheriff watched Clint and Emrys leave town. Satisfied that they were gone, he walked back to his office. From there he saw a man rush down the street toward the livery stable. He recognized the man as Ed Morley, probably the only friend Tom Dover had had in town.

He wondered if he should go to the livery, hold Morley up so Adams and the magician could get a good head start. But that wouldn't matter. Morley would just track them, but he wouldn't try anything until he had help. He wasn't the kind of man to do anything alone—unless he had somehow changed.

The sheriff decided to keep his nose out of it, let the whole matter play out away from him and his town.

FOURTEEN

Clint decided they should travel in a southwesterly direction, the first stop being the town of Kirby, which was growing.

"It's a growing town that's hungering for attention," he told Emrys. "They'd love to have you do a show there."

"Then that is what I shall do."

They traveled most of the day, stopping only for some water. They didn't push the horses hard, so they didn't bother resting them. They would get plenty of rest when they stopped for the night.

When they did stop, Clint took care of the horses while Emrys collected wood and started the fire. While he was rubbing the horses down, he looked over at the camp, saw Emrys standing next to the wood he'd collected. Suddenly, the wood burst into flames. He hadn't seen Emrys strike a match to it. Maybe he'd already lit it, and it hadn't flared up yet. Maybe Emrys knew he was watching, and wanted Clint to think he'd started the fire by using magic.

Clint finished with the horses and came over to the fire.

"I'll make some coffee," he said, "and then we'll have some beans."

"Some of that trail coffee you were telling me about," Emrys said. "This will be very interesting."

Clint boiled the water and then dropped a couple of handfuls of coffee into it. After that he got the beans going in the frying pan. He never said a word to Emrys about how he'd started the fire.

Emrys sat across the fire from Clint and watched him carefully.

"We had a tail today," Clint said.

"What?"

"Somebody was following us."

"I didn't know—how did you know that? Did you see them?" Emrys asked.

"Felt, more than saw."

"How many?"

"Just one, I think."

"So that fellow from town who was friends with the three men I killed," Emrys said. "Why is he following us if he does not have help?"

"I guess he wants to know where we are just in case he does get some help."

"Should we—or you—do something?"

"Why? Let him follow. I don't think he's ever going to find the help he wants. I think the only friends those three really had were those three, and they're dead."

Clint portioned out the beans into two plates, handed one across the fire to Emrys with a fork. Then he poured two cups of coffee and gave the magician one.

"Be careful with that," he said.

Emrys tasted the coffee and his eyebrows went up.

"I have had some potent concoctions in my time, but that is a very strong brew."

Clint sipped his coffee, set it down between his feet, and started eating.

"Tell me about your show," Clint said.

"What do you want to know?"

"Well, what do you do?"

"Magic."

"Yeah, but what kind?" Clint asked. "I've seen some shows in New York and Denver. I saw a man pull a rabbit out of a hat once. Do you do anything like that?"

"A rabbit?" Emrys asked. "From a hat?"

"Supposed to be a pretty good magic trick."

"No, I do not have any rabbits."

"What do you do, then?" Clint asked. "Make flowers appear, like in the sheriff's holster?"

"That was just a little sleight of hand," Emrys said. "Not real magic."

"So what's real magic?" Clint asked. "Come on, show me something."

Emrys studied Clint for a few seconds, chewing his beans, then reached his hands into the fire.

"Hey, what—"

Emrys brought his hand out of the fire. For a moment he seemed unburned, but then Clint saw that the tip of his index finger had a flame on it.

"How—doesn't that burn?"

"No."

"But . . . how?"

Emrys held his finger to his lips and blew out the flame, then picked his fork up from the plate.

"Magic," he said.

Clint had an urge to reach into the fire himself, but he didn't. He could already feel the heat. What would he prove by burning himself?

It had to be some kind of trick.

"Emrys."

"Yes?"

"I think I'm going to watch your show very carefully."

Emrys washed down some beans with coffee and said, "Good."

FIFTEEN

They drove into Kirby before noon, attracting some attention because of Emrys's wagon. But the people were smiling as they rode down the street, happy to see the Magic Man wagon in their town.

Clint and Emrys rode until they came to a livery stable. They stepped down and were met by a tall man in his forties, whose eyes widened when he saw Eclipse.

"Can I help you gents?" he asked.

"We need a place for our horses," Clint said, "and for this wagon."

"Well, I can take the horses, but the wagon would have to go out back."

Clint looked at Emrys.

"It will be protected," the magician assured Clint.

"Okay, then," Clint said to the man. "We'll do it."

"Just drive the wagon around back, and I'll meet you there."

They did as he said, and found him waiting behind the stable for them.

"You can put the wagon there, outside the corral," he said. "I'll take the horses inside."

"Okay," Clint said. "Thanks."

"This is quite a horse," the man said, accepting the reins from Clint.

"Yeah, he is."

Clint and Emrys unhitched the mare from the wagon and handed her over to the hostler when he came back out.

"So what are ya, a magician or somethin'?" he asked.

"Or something," Emrys said.

"You stayin' in town long?"

"Long enough for a show or two," Clint said.

"What's your part in the show?" the man asked.

"Security."

"Oh."

"You got a mayor in this town?" Clint asked.

"No, we don't."

"No mayor?"

"We have a town manager," the man said. "It works better for us."

"So he does the job of a mayor?" Clint asked.

"That's right."

"But you don't call him a mayor."

"No," the hostler said, "town manager. He gets hired, not elected."

"I see."

"You fellas want a hotel, try the Kirby House, down the street. Best in town."

"Thanks," Clint said.

He had removed his saddlebags and rifle before letting the man take Eclipse into the livery.

"Do you need anything from the wagon?" Clint asked.

"Just an extra shirt," Emrys said.

"Well, get it," Clint said. "I'll ask the hostler where we can find this town manager."

Emrys nodded and walked to the wagon.

Clint went in the back door of the livery. He found the man rubbing Eclipse down with obvious relish.

"I never seen a horse this magnificent," he said.

"Just take good care of him."

"Oh, I will."

"Now where do I find this town manager?"

"His name's Paul Wright," the man said, "and he has an office in what used to be City Hall."

"Used to be? What's it called now?"

"Just the Town Hall. Big brick building in the center of town."

"I'll find it," Clint said. "Thanks."

"You gonna do a show?"

"That's what we're going to find out."

He went out back to find Emrys.

They got two rooms at the Kirby House. Clint left his saddlebags and rifle in his room and met up with Emrys again in the lobby.

"Ready?" he asked.

"I'm ready."

"How do you usually do this?"

"I have a meeting to set up a show," Emrys said. "The town gives me a location, and then I walk around town telling people about it."

"Just telling them?"

"Well," he said, "I do what you would call tricks."

"Tricks?"

"No rabbits," he said. "just something to whet the appetite of the people."

"Well, okay," Clint said. "Let's go and find this town manager and get the ball rolling, then."

"Ball?"

"Get things under way," Clint said. "You know, start the—never mind. Let's go."

SIXTEEN

They walked through town, this time not attracting that much attention since they didn't have the wagon—and Eclipse—with them. They were just two men walking down the street, even if one of them was wearing a derby hat.

They found the Town Hall and went inside. There was a collection of doors with writing on them. COUNTY ASSESSOR, TOWN ENGINEER. One just said, ATTORNEY. Then they came to the one that said, TOWN MANAGER. They opened the door and entered.

A woman in her fifties looked up from a desk and watched as they walked in and closed the door behind them.

"Can I help you gentlemen?" she asked.

"Yes, we're here to see Mr. Wright, the town manager," Clint said.

"And what's this about?"

"My friend here is a showman," Clint said. "He would like to put on a show in your town."

"Oh, how wonderful," she said with a smile. "A Wild West Show?"

"No, ma'am," Clint said. "A magic show."

"Magic?"

Emrys produced a bouquet of flowers out of nowhere and handed them to her.

"Why . . . these are real," she said, smelling them.

"Yes, madam," Emrys said. "Very real."

"Wait here," she said. She went into her boss's office behind her, and took the flowers with her. She reappeared in minutes and said, "You can both go in."

"Thank you," Clint said.

They moved past her into the office, and then she closed the door.

The man behind the desk was surprisingly young—in his mid-thirties. He stood and smiled at them. He was wearing a black suit, a boiled white shirt, and a black tie. He looked like a gambler—or a lawyer.

"Gentlemen," he said. "Come in, please. My name is Paul Wright. And you are . . ."

"My name is Clint Adams," Clint said, "and this is Emrys."

"Emrys?" Wright said. "Just Emrys?"

"Just Emrys," Emrys said.

"And you, sir," Wright said, looking at Clint, "are the Gunsmith."

"Guilty as charged."

"Please," Wright said, "sit down and tell me what brings you to Kirby."

They sat and Emrys said, "I wish to perform a show for the people of your town."

"And charge for tickets, I assume."

"Yes," Emrys said, "that is how I make my living."

"Well, I don't see a problem with that," Wright said. "We just have some rules in Kirby about shows."

"What kind of rules?" Clint asked.

"No cure-all tonic sales."

"That is not what I do."

"Yes, my secretary told me you do magic."

"That is correct."

Wright grinned and said, "Rabbit out of a hat and like that?"

Emrys just stared at him.

"No rabbits," Clint said. "This is about real magic."

"Oh, come now, Mr. Adams," Wright said, "don't tell me a man like you believes in real magic?"

"What matters," Clint said, "is what people will believe when they see the show."

Wright stared at Clint, then Emrys, then Clint again.

"So you've seen his tricks?"

"I do not do tricks," Emrys said.

"Look, I mean no disrespect—"

"Mr. Wright," Clint said, "why don't we just discuss the details, and when the time comes, you can see the show and decide for yourself."

"Excellent idea," Wright said. "Tell me what you need for a venue."

At this point, Clint sat back and allowed Emrys to take over.

The town manager was able to let Emrys have an empty lot on a street corner, just off Main Street. Clint and Emrys walked there after their meeting, and Emrys pronounced it perfect for his needs.

"My wagon will fit right in the center, where I can open it to form the stage. And there is plenty of room for the audience."

"I'll tell you what would be perfect for my needs right now," Clint said.

"A steak," Emrys said.

"So now you're a mind reader also?"

"No," Emrys said, "no mind reading necessary. I, too, am hungry."

SEVENTEEN

By the time they got their steaks, the word had spread that there was going to be a show in town.

"Looks like you won't have to walk around town and do much selling," Clint said. "From the conversations going on in here, folks know about it already."

"That is good," Emrys said.

"Can I help you get set up for your show?" Clint asked.

"Yes." They had agreed with the town manager that Emrys would do his show at noon the next day, and again at three. "That would be good."

"Do you need to have any, uh . . ." He almost said "tricks," but Emrys didn't like that word. ". . . magic set up ahead of time?"

"No," Emrys said, "I do not. Everything will be done just at the moment."

"Okay," Clint said. He cut into his mediocre steak and chewed. It was good enough to stop the hungry growling of his stomach, but that was all.

Emrys seemed to have no complaints about the steak,

and ate with great gusto. For a man who seemed to have a voracious appetite, he was surprisingly slim.

After eating, they went back to the empty lot to do some cosmetic work. There was some debris that had to be cleared. While they were doing it, several boys of about eight to ten years old came by to watch.

"Are you the magician?" one of them asked.

"I am," Emrys said.

"Show us some magic," another boy said.

"Come to the show," Emrys told them.

"Aw, yer gonna be sellin' tickets," the third boy said. "We ain't got no money."

"I tell you what," Clint said. "You help us clean this lot, and you can watch the show for free."

"Really?" one of them asked.

"Truly," Emrys said.

Eagerly, the boys ran onto the lot and started to collect debris.

When they were done cleaning up, Emrys took three tickets from his pocket and handed them to the boys.

"Gee, thanks," they yelled.

"Remember," Emrys called as they ran off, "first show at noon."

"How do you sell tickets?" Clint asked as the boys ran off happily.

"On the spot," Emrys said. "That might be something else you can do, if you do not mind. Start selling tickets as soon as the people begin to arrive."

"What about folks trying to watch from across the street, or the rooftops?" Clint asked. "That always seems to be the case with shows like this."

"They will be too far to hear, and to see the subtle nuances of my performance."

"Well, okay," Clint said. "What about putting fliers up around town?"

"It seems to me the word is getting around quite well on its own."

Indeed, more people had stopped to watch what they were doing in the lot, as if they expected some magic to occur at any time.

"Well," Clint said, "we can hit the saloons and talk it up and sell some tickets ahead of time."

"That would be fine," Emrys said. "I can use a cold ale after all this work."

"Let's go, then. We'll just start walking and stop whenever we see a saloon."

"That sounds like a fine idea," Emrys said.

The first saloon they came to was a small one—no gaming, no music, no girls. Just a bartender and about half a dozen customers. They talked up the show, and Emrys managed to sell four tickets with no problem.

The next saloon was larger, with faro and blackjack going on, and two girls working the floor. Still no music, which made it easy for everyone to hear Emrys when he spoke, giving his spiel.

"I ain't buyin' one of your tickets!" a man said from the back.

"Oh?" Emrys asked. "Why is that?"

"Because you're a phony."

"And how can you tell that?" Emrys asked. "You have not yet even seen my performance."

"I don't have to," the man said. "There ain't no such thing as magic."

"Sir, can you step forward so I can see who I am speaking to?" Emrys asked.

The man hesitated, but in the end he moved sheepishly forward, as other men stepped aside to let him through. He was a large man in his forties, looked like he had just come in off the fields.

"What is your name, sir?" Emrys asked.

"Jake Lofton."

"Mr. Lofton, what can I do to convince you to come and see my show?"

"Nothin'," Lofton said. "Yer a phony."

"I assure you, I am not."

"Bah!"

"Come closer, then," Emrys said, "and maybe I can convince you."

Again, Lofton hesitated, but then he shuffled closer to Emrys, eyeing the man suspiciously.

"If I can show you magic right here and now," Emrys asked, "will you buy a ticket?"

Lofton hesitated, looked around, saw that all his friends were watching him.

"I suppose so."

"Bartender," Emrys said, "give my new friend here a cold beer."

The bartender drew a cold one and set it on the bar for Lofton. The man eyed the drink suspiciously, as if he thought Emrys had already done something to it.

"Go ahead," Emrys said, "drink it."

Lofton picked up the beer and sniffed it.

"It is just beer," Emrys said. "The barkeep has just drawn it from the tap."

Lofton looked at the bartender, who said, "Sure thing, Jake."

"And have we ever met before, sir?" Emrys asked Jake, the bartender.

"Ain't never before today," Jake said.

"There you have it," Emrys said. "Why don't you just drink half of it?"

Lofton lifted the beer to his mouth, sniffed at it again, sipped it, found nothing wrong with it, and drank down half of it.

"Now put the mug down and step away from the bar," Emrys instructed.

Lofton did it.

"Now tell everyone how the beer was."

Lofton turned to the people who were watching the action, opened his mouth to speak . . . and his eyes widened when nothing came out.

EIGHTEEN

"Go ahead," Emrys said. "Speak."

Lofton tried again, but not even a croak came out. Just complete silence. Lofton turned to Emrys and began to claw at his throat.

"Now, now," Emrys said to him, "calm down, sir. There is no pain, correct?"

Lofton gave that some thought, then shook his head.

"All right, very good," Emrys said. "No pain. But you cannot speak, is that correct?"

Lofton, still holding his throat, nodded, his eyes wide and panic filled.

"Does anyone here know Mr. Lofton?" Emrys asked. "Just a show of hands, please."

At least half a dozen men raised their hands.

"Have I met him before?" he asked. "Would he be working with me to fool all of you?"

"Not a chance," one man said. "He really thought you was a big phony."

"Good," Emrys said, "good. Mr. Lofton, are you ready to buy a ticket?"

Lofton, eyes still wide, clawed at his throat again.

"If I give you back your voice, will you buy a ticket, sir?"

Lofton nodded jerkily. He would have done anything to get his voice back.

"All right, then," Emrys said. "Please drink the remainder of the beer."

Lofton blinked, picked up the mug, sniffed it again, then drank it down.

"There," Emrys said. "Will you buy a ticket?"

Lofton touched his throat and said, "Uh, uh, oh . . . I can talk!"

The other men in the saloon looked on in awe, and then began to applaud.

"I—I'll buy a ticket," Lofton said.

"Me, too," another man said.

"And me!"

Men stepped forward, each waving a dollar for a ticket to the Magic Man's show.

After Clint and Emrys left the saloon, Clint asked, "Okay, how did you do that?"

"I did nothing," Emrys said.

"You struck that man dumb!"

"Oh, that?" Emrys said. "He did that himself. All I did was buy him a beer."

"Wait. You're telling me that wasn't magic?"

"Why, Clint," Emrys said, "you don't believe in magic."

"So he really could talk?"

"If he wanted to."

"But . . . he tried, and he couldn't."

"He was convinced that I was going to do something," Emrys said.

"So then . . . that was a trick?" Clint asked. "Like . . . mind over matter?"

"Something like that."

"That was amazing!"

"And it sold a lot of tickets," Emrys said. "You chose a good town, my friend. I think perhaps together you and I are going to do well."

"I think we got a couple more saloons to hit before we turn in," Clint said. "And after what you did in that last one, the word is bound to spread."

"That is excellent," Emrys said. "Let us then continue on!"

NINETEEN

They sold a bunch of tickets in the other two saloons, and returned to their hotel.

"We did pretty well," Clint said.

"For a start," Emrys said. "We will have to rise early in the morning to sell more, and then you will sell more just before the show."

"Suits me," Clint said. "As long as I get breakfast before you put me to work."

"Steak and eggs, correct?"

"Correct."

"I will meet you down here early," Emrys said. "We still have some work to do to get ready."

Clint knew that. At the very least they had to fetch the wagon from the livery and get it set up in the middle of the empty lot.

The hotel had a dining room, so they figured to try breakfast there, since the steak they'd had earlier was basically edible.

"Remember," Clint said as they went up the stairs, "stay away from your window, and be careful answering your door. If someone knocks, it won't be me, and it won't be a pretty girl. Got it?"

"I understand," Emrys said. "But do you still think that man is watching us?"

"I know he is," Clint said.

Clint left the magician at his door and went down the hall to his own room.

In his room, Emrys used the pitcher and basin to wash his face and his bare chest, paying special attention to his armpits.

So far Kirby looked promising, as did Clint Adams as a magician's assistant.

He dried off and walked to the bed, where he sat and closed his eyes. Anybody watching him would think that he had fallen asleep, but in truth he had put himself into a trancelike state. Slowly, he keeled over until he was lying on his side on the bed.

He would not open his eyes again until morning.

Clint likewise washed up in his room, then went to the bed, sat, and pulled off his boots. He took a copy of *Le Morte d'Arthur* by Sir Thomas Malory out of his saddlebags. He'd been carrying the book around for a while, but had yet not had the chance to begin reading it. He thought tonight was as good a time as any.

He had heard the legend of King Arthur and the Knights of the Round Table, but had never read about them. He did so this night, and found it not only interesting, but kind of enlightening.

Ed Morley followed Clint and the magician from saloon to saloon while they sold tickets for the show. He watched through a window as the magician did one of his tricks, and ended up selling a bunch of tickets in one saloon. He then followed them to their hotel.

When he was sure the two men were in for the night, he turned and went back to the saloon where the magic man had performed his trick. Maybe he could find some help there.

Clint knew they were still being followed. But there was still no harm being done by the man. As long as he had no one to back his play, he would be no danger. So Clint sat on his bed, quite content to read about King Arthur, the Knights . . . and Merlin, possibly the greatest magician—or wizard—ever known.

TWENTY

Clint woke at first light, found himself rested and ready to rise. Once again he used the pitcher and basin to wash up, then donned a clean shirt, strapped on his gun. And left the room. He found Emrys in the lobby, looking even more well rested then he was.

"Did you sleep well?" Clint asked.

"Extremely well," Emrys said. "And you?"

"I read for a while, then went to sleep and didn't wake until morning."

"You read?" Emrys asked. "What are you reading?"

"*Le Morte d'Arthur.*"

"Ah, Thomas Malory's tale of King Arthur."

"You know it?" Clint asked.

"Oh, very well," Emrys said as they entered the dining room. "Well enough to know that Malory almost had it right."

"Almost?"

"Well, you know, authors and their books. They always employ a certain amount of poetic license."

"Which parts did he have wrong?"

"Oh, just some relationship things," Emrys said. "Arthur and Guinevere, Guinevere and Lancelot, Arthur and Modred, Arthur and Morgana . . . oh, and that business about the Holy Grail."

As they sat down, Clint laughed and said, "Those are all the major plotlines of the book."

"Indeed," Emrys said, "plotlines, as in fiction."

"You're saying Malory's version of Arthur and the Knights is fiction?"

"No," Emrys said, "I simply said that Sir Thomas employed a bit of poetic license in his telling. After all, Clint, how many of the stories about you are true?"

"Not many."

"Exactly," Emrys said. "It is the stuff of legends."

A waiter came over and took their order.

"Why don't you tell me the real story, then?" Clint asked.

"I think," Emrys said, "we should save that for a night on the trail, don't you?"

"I suppose."

"We must go to the livery today to fetch the wagon to the empty lot," Emrys said. "It must be placed just so."

"I'll leave that to you," Clint said. "I'll follow where you lead."

"Excellent."

The steak and eggs came, and the steaks were cooked much better than the ones they'd had the night before. The meal was good enough for them to forgo any further conversation.

After breakfast they walked to the livery, circled around to the back, where the wagon was.

"It looks secure," Clint said. "I was afraid someone would break in."

"I told you," Emrys said. "It is protected."

"Yes, you did tell me that," Clint said. "I just don't know by what." Emrys opened his mouth to answer and Clint cut him off. "I know, I know . . . magic!"

"We'll need to hitch the horse up to take it to the lot," Emrys said.

"I'll get her," Clint said.

"Good," Emrys said. "I'll take the protection off so we can move the wagon."

"You do that."

Clint went into the livery, found the stall with the mare in it, put a bridle on her, and walked her out to the wagon. They removed the bridle and hitched her to the wagon.

"Is everything set?" Clint asked.

"Most of my preparation will happen when we get to the lot," Emrys said.

"Okay, then. Can I ride with you?" Clint asked, not sure if Emrys would allow him on the wagon.

"Of course."

They climbed aboard, and Emrys shook the reins at the mare.

People were already gathered at the lot for the performance.

As Emrys climbed down from the wagon, he said to Clint, "Perhaps you can find out how many of them already have tickets, and how many wish to buy some?"

"I can do that."

While Emrys went around to the back of the wagon, opened the doors, and climbed in, Clint approached the crowd of people. About half of them had tickets, so he got busy selling tickets to the other half.

Standing in at the back of the crowd was Ed Morley. The night before he had not managed to find anyone in the saloon

willing to listen to him. All he had left to do was watch the
magician's show, until he could figure something out.

The Gunsmith did not seem to recognize him when he
paid for his ticket.

Clint, however, recognized Morley immediately. So now he
knew who'd been trailing them the whole time. The man
had had a big mouth in Ten Sleep, but he obviously had little
more than that going for him.

While he was selling tickets, Clint saw the side wall of
the wagon come down to form a stage for Emrys. The side
of the wagon was covered by a curtain, which Emrys would
appear from behind.

At that moment, Clint saw Paul Wright, the town manager.

"Good morning, Mr. Wright."

"Mr. Adams," Wright said. "I'm looking forward to this
show."

"I hope you enjoy it."

"I hope you don't mind, but I brought along our town
sheriff, just to be sure there's no trouble."

"That's fine," Clint said, looking at the man with Wright.
He was tall, craggy-faced, looked like he'd spent most of
his life working outdoors.

"Sheriff Harve Greely," he said. "Good to meet you,
Adams."

"Likewise, Sheriff."

"I can buy a ticket for the sheriff," Wright said.

"I don't think that's necessary," Clint said, "since the
sheriff's just here doing his job."

"No, no," Wright said, pushing the money at Clint, "I
always like to support the performing arts."

"All right," Clint said, taking the money. "Thanks."

The crowd continued to grow as other ticket holders appeared. When it seemed to him that everyone there had a ticket, Clint turned and walked to the wagon.

"Are you in there?" Clint called through the curtain.

"Where else would I be, my friend?" Emrys asked.

"These people are ready for you."

"All right," Emrys said. "Perhaps you should stand back."

Not knowing what to expect, Clint hurriedly did just that.

TWENTY-ONE

With a great puff of smoke, Emrys appeared, clad in a burgundy robe.

Clint never saw him step out from behind the smoke. He actually seemed to appear from the smoke itself. It was a neat trick to begin with—but he wouldn't say that to the magician.

"Ladies and gentlemen," Emrys said, "gather round, please. Yes, yes, come closer and you will see feats of magic that will surprise and amaze you."

Reluctantly, the people began to come closer. The puff of smoke had already surprised them.

For the next half hour, Emrys performed magic that drew oohs and ahhs from the crowd, including Clint. As closely as he watched, he could not figure out how the man was doing it. He made things disappear, he made them float in the air, he made them reappear.

He drew people up onstage, strangers, and was able to make things appear in and disappear from their pockets.

"Sheriff," Emrys said, spotting the lawman, "why don't you come up here and help me with something?"

"Sure, why not?" the lawman asked.

Emrys had a movable set of steps next to the stage so people could climb up. The lawman walked up and stood next to the magician, looking uncomfortable.

"How have you enjoyed the show so far?" he asked.

"It amazin'," the lawman said. "I don't know how you do the things you do."

"Well, that is the point," Emrys said, "for people to be amazed. Now, how many people out there know the sheriff?"

Almost all the people raised their hands.

"Very good, then you know that the sheriff is not in league with me."

Most of the people frowned and looked confused, so Clint said, "He means the sheriff isn't in cahoots with him."

That the people understood.

"Yes, that is it," Emrys said. "Cahoots." He looked at the lawman. "Sheriff, can I borrow your badge?"

"My badge?"

"Yes," Emrys said, "I assure you, you will get it back."

"Well, all right." The lawman took the badge off and handed it to Emrys.

"Thank you," Emrys said, holding the tin in the palm of one hand. "Now, do you all see the badge?" He held it up so that the midday sun reflected off it.

The people nodded and spoke their assent.

"Good," Emrys said, "watch closely."

He closed his hand over the badge, held his fist aloft, and then opened his hand.

The badge was gone.

The crowd oohed and ahhed again.

"Sonofabitch," the sheriff said. "Where's my badge?"

"Don't worry, Sheriff," Emrys said, "it's right here." He opened his other hand—which was empty.

"It ain't there," the lawman said.

"What?" Emrys looked at his left hand. "Well, that is a surprise."

"Where is it?" the sheriff asked. "Hey, I'm responsible for that badge. If you lose it, I have to buy another one."

"Hmm," Emrys said, "I am sorry to hear that. Well, perhaps that fellow will give you his."

Emrys pointed to a man standing in front, who was wearing a leather vest over a blue shirt.

"What? Who?" the sheriff asked.

"That fellow with the blue shirt."

"That's Herb Ripkin," the sheriff said. "He ain't no lawman. He don't have a badge."

"Really?" Emrys said. "Well, Mr. Ripkin, can you come up here, please?"

"Huh? Me?"

"Yes, sir, please," Emrys said. "Come on up."

Reluctantly the man moved toward the stage. Clint pointed at the stairs and Ripkin climbed.

"Come right over here," Emrys said.

Ripkin moved past the sheriff to stand next to Emrys.

"Are you sure you are not wearing a badge?"

"I ain't got no badge."

"No?" Emrys reached over and moved aside the man's vest, looking on both sides of his shirt. "I was sure you did."

"Hey, Magic Man," the sheriff said, "where's my badge?"

"Well, maybe . . ." Emrys looked down into the crowd, spotted a pretty young lady in a green dress. "She has it," he said, pointing.

"What?" she said.

Everyone turned and looked at her.

"That's Sally Prescott," the lawman said. "She don't have my badge."

"She does," Emrys insisted.

"I do not!" Sally said.

"Madam," Emrys said, "if you would check beneath your skirts."

"What?" she said indignantly. "I would never . . ." She stopped short, as if she suddenly realized something. "Wait . . ." She reached down to her skirt, then said, "There's something . . ." She lifted her skirt to show the white undergarment beneath, and there, pinned to it, was the sheriff's badge.

"Oh my God!" she said. She unpinned the badge, dropped her skirt down, and then came forward to hold the badge out to the sheriff, who reached down and took it.

"It's my badge, all right," he said.

The assembled crowd broke into wild applause, including the embarrassed, but impressed, Sally.

The sheriff and Ripkin stepped down from the stage, and Emrys took a bow and announced that the show was over. He proceeded to disappear in a puff of smoke.

"That was quite entertaining," Paul Wright said to Clint a few moments later.

"Yes," Clint said, "it was pretty good."

"I wonder how he got young Sally to go along with that."

"You think he knew Sally? That she was working with him?" Clint asked.

"Well, how else would the badge have gotten beneath her skirts?" the man asked.

"What about the sheriff?" Clint asked. "Was he also working with him?"

"Well, we only have the sheriff's word that the badge was his," Wright said.

"Mr. Wright," Clint said, "I think you better talk to your lawman and Miss Sally about your theory."

"Perhaps I will," Wright said. "Will the three o'clock show be the same?"

"Damned if I know," Clint said. "He doesn't keep me that informed."

"Well," Wright said, "perhaps I'll come and watch that one, too."

"You do that, sir," Clint said.

Wright nodded, turned, and walked over to the sheriff.

TWENTY-TWO

As the crowd dispersed, Clint walked to the back of the wagon. The doors were closed. He tried them and found them locked. He walked around to the stage portion again, but Emrys had already pulled it up.

"Emrys!" he called. "You still in there?" He went around back and banged on the doors.

He waited and after a moment he heard the doors start to open. In moments Emrys had stepped down. The robe was gone, and he was wearing trousers and a shirt again.

"That was great," Clint said.

"How did the people like it?"

"They ate it up."

"Good."

"How did you do that?"

"Do what?" Emrys Asked. "You will have to be more specific."

"The thing with the badge," Clint said. "That fellow Wright is convinced the sheriff and the girl, Sally, were working with you."

"Well, I hope he talks to them and finds out they were not," Emrys said.

"That's what I told him to do."

"Excellent."

"But how did you do it?"

"You were watching," Emrys said. "You could not tell?"

"I couldn't tell how you did any of it!"

"Well, that is good," Emrys said. "If you could tell me how I did it, I would think you were a wizard."

"Wizard?"

"Magician," Emrys said hastily. "I meant magician."

"You mean a wizard . . . like Merlin?"

"I need to get ready for the three o'clock performance," Emrys said.

"By doing what?"

"A couple of things I did were kind of sloppy."

"Like what?"

"Well, for one, the badge."

"What about it?"

"It was supposed to be on the chest of the man with the vest," Emrys said.

"So how did it get under the girl's skirts?" Clint asked.

"I do not know."

Clint stared at Emrys.

"You losing control of your magic?" he asked.

"Well," Emrys said, "magic is really not supposed to exist here."

"Here? You mean, in the West?"

"I mean—yes, yes, I mean here, in the West."

"Well, what would you like me to do?"

"I could use some lunch," Emrys said. "Could you go and bring back some sandwiches?"

"Sure," Clint said, "why not?"

* * *

Clint walked until he came to a small café. When he went inside, the first person he saw was the waitress—who was Sally, from the magic trick with the badge.

"Hello," he said.

She turned and stared at him, wide-eyed.

"Did he send you?" she asked.

"Who?"

"Him. The magician."

"Uh, yeah, but only for some sandwiches."

"Oh, well, all right," she said. "What kind?"

"Do you have ham?"

"Yes," she said. "How many would you like?"

"I'll take four."

The other diners in the place watched Clint while he spoke to Sally, and then after she went into the kitchen. Rather than staying there to be stared at, Clint stepped outside. Sally eventually came out with a bag filled with sandwiches.

"Thank you," he said. "What do I owe you?"

"Nothing," she said. "Can you tell me how he did it?"

"Did what?"

"The trick," she said. "With the badge. Can you tell me how he got it pinned beneath my . . . my skirt?"

"Oh, I don't know how he does his magic," Clint said. He held up the bag. "I just get him his sandwiches."

"I just . . ." she said, shaking her head. "I just can't figure it out."

"Why try?" he asked. "It was a trick. Let it go at that."

"But . . . but how did he get the badge under my skirt without me feeling it?"

"I don't know, Sally."

She turned and went back into the cafe, shaking her pretty head. Clint hoped she'd be able to get over it.

TWENTY-THREE

Clint returned with the sandwiches. Once again he had to call out to Emrys to come out of the wagon. He heard footsteps inside as if the magician was coming from a long way off, then the doors opened and he came out. Cliff handed him two of the sandwiches, and they sat down on the edge of the wagon to eat.

"Ah," the magician said, taking a bite, "this is very good."

"We'll have to drink water," Clint said. There was a barrel of water attached to the side of the wagon.

"No matter," Emrys said, "these sandwiches and water will make an excellent meal."

"Have you figured out what hap—I mean, the problems with your—I mean—"

"Yes," Emrys said, "I know what I did wrong with the badge. But I will do something else at three o'clock. Perhaps the sheriff will not be there."

"That's true."

"Our friend was watching your show," Clint said.

"Our friend?"

"The man who followed us from Ten Sleep."

"Truly?"

"Maybe," Clint said, "if he's there again this afternoon, you should bring him up onstage."

"That would be . . . funny," Emrys said.

"Yes, it would be," Clint said. "If he is there, I will point him out."

"Excellent."

They finished their sandwiches, washed them down with water.

"I'm going to walk around town and see if I can drum up some more customers for the three o'clock show."

They had collected all the tickets from the morning crowd, so they had them to sell again for the three o'clock performance.

"Oh, by the way," I said, "I think you may have done Sally some harm."

"In what way?"

"Well, I saw her when I bought the sandwiches. She was the waitress. She's very concerned about how you got that badge underneath her skirts."

"Did you assure her it was magic?"

"I assured her that it was something she was never going to be able to explain, but she didn't seem able to accept that."

"I am sorry," Emrys said. "I did not mean to do that."

"Just don't pick any more young women."

"Understood."

"Okay."

Clint took a bunch of the tickets and left to start selling.

Mostly stopping in the saloons again, as well as some cafés and stores, he managed to get rid of all the tickets. It helped that word had gotten around about the early performance. Many of the people who had attended the early show also bought tickets for the afternoon show.

Clint came across the three boys who had helped them clear the lot, and realized they had not attended the early show.

"What happened to you guys?"

Mournfully, one of them said, "We had chores to do and we didn't finish in time."

"Well, do you still have your tickets?"

They nodded.

"Then you can still come," Clint said. "The tickets will be good."

"Yay!" the boys shouted, running off happily.

"See you there, boys," he called out after them.

When Clint returned to the wagon, Emrys was nowhere to be seen, so he assumed that the magician was inside. The crowd was due to begin arriving shortly.

"Emrys!" he shouted, banging on the doors. "I'm back!"

Once again he heard those odd echoing footsteps, and then the doors opened and Emrys stepped out.

"All the tickets are gone," Clint said. "Looks like you'll have another good crowd at three o'clock."

"Good."

"Are you ready?"

"I am very ready," Emrys said. "Would you like to participate?"

"In what way?"

"Oh, we could incorporate something with your guns, if you like," Emrys said.

"I don't think so," Clint said. "I spent some time with Buffalo Bill's show and didn't like it much. Besides, if you wanted some sharpshooting done, you could probably do it yourself."

"Oh, I doubt I could match your prowess with a pistol," Emrys said.

"Not even if you used magic?"

"Well, yes, in that case I could," Emrys said. "But without magic, your marksmanship is much superior to mine."

"Well," Clint said, "I don't know if I want to test that fact. Not after seeing you shoot it out with those three."

"That was not only magic, Clint," Emrys said, "that was luck."

"I'm not so sure about that," Clint said. He saw that people were starting to crowd around them. "I guess you better get inside and open up your stage. I'll let you know when the crowd's all here."

"Excellent," he said.

As the magician began to climb back into the wagon, Clint said, "Have a good show."

Emrys stopped for a moment, looked at Clint, said, "Thank you," and climbed in.

On a rooftop across the street, Ed Morley sighted down the barrel of his rifle, aiming at the magician's wagon. If he fired at that moment, he felt sure he could put a bullet in the middle of the c in MAGIC MAN. It should be just as easy to put a bullet into the magician's chest. After that, it would be a matter of choosing the right time to try for the Gunsmith.

He settled in while the crowd gathered, patiently waiting for the show to begin.

TWENTY-FOUR

The show went off without a hitch.

Emrys had all his ducks in a row, amazed the crowd at every turn. The sheriff did not return, so there was no badge trick. Sally also did not return, so there was no embarrassment for her—or any other woman, for that matter. Emrys stayed away from skirts this time.

The town manager, Paul Wright, was there again, apparently enjoying the show, and the three boys showed up and were wide-eyed the entire time.

The levitation "tricks" were of particular interest to Clint. Emrys took apparently solid objects and made them float in the air. There was no question of any kind of strings being attached, for there was nothing above them to attach a string to. This was the only thing he thought he'd press the magician to show him. He really wanted to know how it was done.

There were no hecklers, which was surprising. Both shows had gone off without any real trouble.

So far.

*   *   *

From the roof, Morley watched Emrys perform his show. He was trying to wait for the right moment to fire, sighting down the barrel of the rifle. A time or two he had to wipe a sweat drop from the tip of his nose, or dry his hands on his thighs.

This was no longer a matter of getting revenge for Tom Dover and the others. Hell, they weren't really that close as friends. No, this was about Emrys, and who he was.

Morley was convinced that Emrys was the Devil—well, an emissary of the Devil. If he was the actual Devil, then a bullet wouldn't kill him.

But this man would be killed by a bullet right to the chest.

And the moment was now.

Emrys completed his performance and, just prior to disappearing in a puff of smoke, spread his arms wide to the crowd.

Clint heard the shot and saw the bullet strike Emrys squarely in the chest.

There were some screams as Emrys staggered back and fell into the wagon. Moments later the stage folded up, closing the wagon.

Clint, meanwhile, was busy checking the storefronts and rooftops across the street for the shooter. He thought he saw someone on one of the roofs and broke into a run, yelling, "Somebody call the doctor!"

He pushed through the crowd and ran across the street. He found an alley and used it to get to the back of the buildings, hoping he'd catch the shooter back there. When he got there, it was deserted. He didn't know which back door matched the building he thought he'd seen the shooter on. The dirt was filled with tracks, but no way to tell the shooter's from anyone else's.

There was nothing he could do, so he ran back to the wagon. The crowd was milling around, as if unsure of what to do. From the sound of it, some of them thought this was part of the show, and that the magician might appear unharmed, to amaze them again. Clint knew this was not part of the show at all.

"Did anyone send for the doctor?" he demanded.

"Yes," Paul Wright said, "the doctor and the sheriff."

At that moment the lawman came running up to them with another man in tow. He was middle-aged, dressed in a suit and carrying a black bag.

"Adams, this is Doc Mitchell," the sheriff said.

"Who got shot?" the doctor asked.

"The magician," Wright said.

"Where is he?" the doctor asked, looking around.

"In there," Wright said, pointing to the wagon.

"What's he doin' in there?"

"The bullet made him fall back into the wagon," Wright said, "and then the flap went up. He's inside."

"Come on," Clint said. "The doors are in the back."

He led them to the rear of the wagon, where they tried the doors and found them locked.

"How do we get in?" the doctor asked.

"He has to let us in," Clint said.

"How can he do that if he's dead?" the sheriff asked. "The man who came to fetch me said he'd been shot square in the chest."

"Sheriff," Clint said, "the shot came from one of those rooftops. Maybe you can have a look up there."

"The shooter's certainly gone," the lawman said, "but I'll have a look."

He walked off, leaving Clint, Paul Wright, and Doc Mitchell at the rear of the wagon.

"We have to get in there," the doctor said. "He could be bleeding to death and not able to open it."

Clint stepped forward and began to bang on the doors.

"Emrys! Are you all right?" he shouted and banged his fist on the doors harder. "Emrys, open up!"

"His name is Emrys?" the doctor asked in surprise.

"Well, yeah," Clint said. "That's the name we know him by."

"Why?" Wright asked. "Does that mean something to you?"

"Are either of you up on your Knights of the Round Table history?" the doc asked.

"I'm reading Thomas Malory's book now," Clint said.

"I don't know if this is in the Malory book," the doctor said, "but there are some sources that mentioned Merlin's last name being . . . Emrys."

Clint and Wright stared at the doctor, and just at that moment they heard the doors unlock, and saw them swing open.

TWENTY-FIVE

"What the hell—" Wright said as Emrys stepped out.

"What is all the fuss?" he asked. His robes were gone, and he was once again wearing a shirt and trousers.

A gasp went up from the crowd as he appeared.

"Mr. Wright," Clint said, "maybe we should get this crowd to disperse. We don't know that there's not going to be any more shooting."

Wright looked around for the sheriff, then said, "All right, I'll do it."

"Sir," Doc Mitchell said, "I was summoned here because these people saw you shot in the chest."

"Shot in the chest?" Emrys asked. "I feel rather well for a man who was shot in the chest, Doctor."

"Nevertheless," Mitchell said, "I am here and I would like to examine you."

"As you wish, Doctor."

"Can we go inside the wagon?"

"I am afraid not," Emrys said. "If you want to examine me, it will have to be right here."

"Very well," the doctor put down his bag. "Remove your shirt, please."

Emrys sat on the back step of the wagon, unbuttoned his shirt, and took it off. Clint kept quiet about what he had seen, but he was with the rest of the crowd. The magician had been shot in the chest, and yet there were no marks there. Nothing.

The doctor examined Emrys's chest and said, "I can't see any sign that this man was shot."

"As I told you," Emrys said.

"What happened, Emrys?" Clint asked. "There was a shot and you fell back."

"Obviously," Emrys said, "he missed, but I was startled and stumbled back. Then I pulled the flap up to keep him from shooting again."

Most of the crowd had dispersed, but the people who were still there were gawking at Emrys. Clint heard somebody say, "See, I told you it was part of the show."

Paul Wright wrangled the rest of the crowd away from the wagon and got them to move on. He then rejoined the other men.

"Paul, I don't appreciate being called out for no reason," the doctor complained.

"Sorry, Doc," Wright said. "I really thought the man had been shot."

"Doctor, please," Emrys said, "I'm sure the people who sent for you were only trying to help. I will happily pay you for your time."

"Never mind," the doctor said. "I'm glad you weren't shot, sir, and I don't hold you responsible for this." He looked at Wright and pointed his finger. "The city will get my bill."

"Fine," Wright said, "we'll pay it."

The doctor stalked away, leaving Clint, Wright, and Emrys.

"Well, gentleman," Wright said, "if that was part of the show, it was very convincing."

"I am glad you enjoyed the show again," Emrys said.

"Will you want the lot again tomorrow?" Wright asked.

"No, sir," Emrys said. "I perform for one day only, and then I move on. We will be leaving town tomorrow."

"Okay, then," Wright said, shaking both their hands. "It's been . . . interesting."

As Wright walked away, Clint said, "Yeah, very interesting."

"Why are you looking at me that way?" Emrys asked.

"I saw you shot in the chest," Clint said. "I saw the blood."

"I told you, Clint," Emrys said, "he missed. Whoever it was, he missed."

"Where's your robe?"

"What?"

"The robe you were wearing," Clint said. "I want to see it."

"Why?"

"Because it's probably soaked with blood."

"It's not."

"Let me see it, then."

"Clint—"

"Emrys!" I said. "You know what I found out today. That's Merlin's last name. Is that why you took the name? To name yourself after Merlin?"

Emrys didn't answer.

"Okay," Clint said, "let's put that question aside for the moment. Let me see the robe. If there's no blood on it, I'll drop the whole thing. Except for the shooter. I'm going to try to find him."

"My robe."

"Yes."

"Very well," Emrys said. "I will get it."

He opened the doors to the wagon. The interior looked completely dark to Clint; he could make out nothing. Emrys went inside, closed the doors behind him, reappeared moments later with a robe balled up in his hands.

"There, satisfied?"

Clint took the robe, shook it out, and held it in front of him. He turned it both ways, looked at the front and back. No holes, and no blood. He handed it back to Emrys.

"I guess I have to be."

Emrys opened the doors again and tossed the robe inside, then closed them.

"Wait a minute," Clint said. "How many of those do you have?"

"I have one," Emrys said. "One robe. The one I was wearing."

"Okay," Clint said, "okay. Let's move on."

"That is what I want to do," Emrys said. "I will take the wagon and the horse back to the livery stable. And we will leave town tomorrow."

"I'll go with you."

"I thought you wanted to look for the shooter."

"I do," Clint said. "It's got to be the same man who's been following us."

"The one you said was no danger."

"Well," Clint said, "if he missed, then I guess I was right."

TWENTY-SIX

Morley was convinced that he had killed the magician until he heard the talk in the saloon.

"Musta been part of the show," someone said. "Sure looked like the bullet hit him in the chest, but there he was, walkin' around a few minutes later, just fine."

Had he missed? He didn't think so. As far as he knew, the bullet had hit the magician in the chest.

"What'll ya have?" the bartender asked.

His intention had been to have a beer, but he said, "Whiskey."

This wasn't right. First the man outdraws three men cleanly, as if by magic, and now this.

The Devil, that's what he was.

The Devil.

Clint walled Emrys over to the livery with the wagon and the mare. They put the wagon back where it had been, and Clint walked the mare into the stable, rubbed her down, and fed her.

"Okay," he said, coming back out. "That's done."

"Now what?" Emrys asked.

"Now you go back to your hotel room and—"

"I know," he said. "Stay away from the window."

"Well, now that someone actually has taken a shot at you, definitely yes. And don't answer the door."

"Since the bullet obviously missed me," Emrys said, "what if he was shooting at you?"

"If someone was shooting at me," Clint said, "I'd know it."

Emrys didn't argue.

They walked to the hotel together and Clint stopped in the lobby.

"What are you going to do?" Emrys asked.

"I'm going to walk around town, see what I can scare up."

"What do you hope to scare up?"

"Information, hopefully," Clint said. "And maybe I can get the shooter to make a try for me."

"And miss again, I hope."

"Exactly," Clint said, "but I won't miss."

"You're going to kill him?"

"If I can," Clint said. "Better than him killing me, or you."

"I have to agree there."

"Remember," Clint said, "keep clear of the wagon."

"I will certainly remember."

Clint stood there and watched Emrys go up the stairs to his room, then he turned and left the hotel.

Clint tried a few saloons, where he heard people talking about the incidents of the afternoon. Most people seemed to think the shooting was part of the act. And they thought it was pretty damn good.

But he knew there was one man in town who didn't think it was good.

Clint had a beer in the third saloon. How was he going to pick the shooter out? He should have paid more attention to him on the trail, doubled back to take a look at him, but he was convinced at that point that the man was no danger.

Some of the customers in the saloon with him looked nervous, but he had learned long ago that he had that effect on certain men.

He was finishing up his beer when the sheriff walked in, came to the bar to join him.

"Sheriff," Clint said, nodding. "Beer?"

"I have a standin' order," the lawman said as the bartender handed him one.

"Oh."

The lawman sipped his beer and said, "So everyone I've talked to who saw the shooting says the magician was shot in the chest. What do you say?"

"It certainly looked that way to me."

"But he's unharmed."

"Obviously."

"What do you make of it?" the sheriff asked. "Magic?"

"You know," Clint said, "a few days ago I'd have said no."

"What do you say now?"

"Now I say . . . maybe."

"I still don't believe in magic," the man said. "Let's talk about something we both believe in."

"The shooter?"

The sheriff nodded.

"I checked the rooftops, found some scuff marks, and a spent cartridge for a Winchester. You didn't even get half a good look at 'im?"

"Just a glance as he pulled back from the roof," Clint said. "I ran across the street, but found nothing. I know we were followed from Ten Sleep, but I didn't think he had this in him."

"Well, if he had it in him this time," the sheriff said, "maybe he'll try again."

"Maybe."

"Are you sure he tried for the magician and not you?" the lawman asked. "I mean, that would make more sense."

"If he tried for me, then he's a terrible shot," Clint said. "He missed by a mile."

"Well, watch your back," the sheriff said. He drank half his beer and put the mug down. "Gotta make my rounds. Paul Wright says you're leavin' in the mornin'."

"That's right."

"Well, do me a favor—try not to get killed, or kill anybody, until then."

"I'll do my best, Sheriff."

TWENTY-SEVEN

Clint went back to his hotel. When he got to his room, he sidled up to the window so he could peer out. The problem was, he didn't feel eyes on his back anymore. Now he was looking across the street, hoping to spot somebody watching the hotel, but nobody was there.

He had allowed this to go on too long, because his attention had been on Emrys and his strange behavior. His "magic." Because of that, Emrys—or even he himself—might have been killed this afternoon.

So he had to forget about whether Emrys's magic was real or not. The bullet that had been fired was real, and he had to find the man who'd fired it. That probably wasn't going to happen in town, though. Since the shooter missed, he'd probably follow them when they left Kirby. So his identity was going to be discovered out on the trail, and not in town.

Morley was in Kirby's whorehouse.

He decided he needed some relaxation. Once he was relaxed, he could make a decision about his next move. He was too wound up at the moment, especially after missing his shot—if he had missed.

In the parlor of the whorehouse he picked out a little Chinese gal and went upstairs with her. She was the only Chinese he saw in the place, and he had a liking for their long, straight black hair and their almond-shaped eyes.

"What you like?" she asked him, sitting on the bed next to him.

"I want to relax," he said.

"I can give you massage," she said. "That make you relax."

"A massage?" he said. "I don't even know what that is."

"I show you," she said. "You get naked."

She didn't have to tell him twice. He took off all his clothes, dropped his gun belt on the floor next to the bed. When he grabbed for her, she slapped his hands away.

"Hey!" he said.

"You not touch me," she said. "I touch you."

"Well, okay," he said.

"Lay down."

He lay down on his back, his hard cock already jutting up from his groin.

"Hmm," she said, stroking it with her long nails so that it jumped, "I take care of that later. You roll over."

He rolled onto his stomach.

She stood next to the bed, unbelted the filmy robe she was wearing, and let it drop to the floor. He turned his head so he could see her small, brown-tipped breasts and the black patch of hair between her legs.

"Now you relax," she said, climbing onto the bed with him.

She straddled him so that he felt the coarse pubic hair on his bare butt. He was about to say "the hell with it" and flip over when she started leaning on him, kneading his flesh, rubbing his back.

"Oh, yeah . . ." he said.

"That good, right?" she asked.

"That's very good."

Her perfume filled his head; her touch eased all the stress out of his muscles. She used her palms, the heels of her hands, her pointy elbows, and even her hard nipples. Morley was excited, but he was also drifting off, he was that relaxed.

"Oh yeah," he said again . . .

Clint decided to go to one of the saloons and have a beer. He chose one of the smaller ones, so there'd be less to distract him.

He ordered a beer, and when the bartender set it down in front of him, he asked, "Hey, ain't you with that magic guy?"

"I am."

"Say, is he really doin' magic?"

"That's what he says."

"Yeah, but whatta you say?"

Clint sipped his beer and said, "I'm like everybody else, friend. I'm watching and wondering."

"I thought you was partners."

"No," Clint said, "I'm just traveling with him for a while."

"So he don't tell you how them tricks work?"

"He doesn't tell me anything," Clint said.

"Huh," the man said, and moved on down the bar.

Clint used the mirror behind the bar to look at the room. He was being watched, possibly because of who he was, but more likely because of Emrys. It all seemed to be idle curiosity, though. From years of experience, he knew when trouble was looking for him, and he didn't have that feeling here.

He finished his beer, decided to go back to the hotel to see if Emrys wanted to get something to eat.

The Chinese whore said her name was Ling. It sounded like a stupid name to Morley, but that was how those Chinese girls were.

She continued to work on his upper back, his lower back, eventually began to knead the muscles in his butt, and then his thighs.

At that point she reached between his thighs to touch his balls, stroke them, then reached farther and took hold of his hard cock.

"Now you turn over," she said huskily.

He rolled over and she moved up on him, braced her hands on his belly, and rubbed her coarse pubic hair up and down the length of his cock. As she did that, she grew wet, wetting him at the same time.

"Goddamnit!" he said in awe. She was like magic.

She lifted her hips, reached between them, grabbed his cock, and held it so she could sit on it. The spongy head of his penis slid right into her, and she sat down on him, taking the length of him inside.

"You relax," she told him again, "and I do all the work."

He didn't argue . . .

TWENTY-EIGHT

Clint and Emrys ate supper in the hotel dining room.

"No point in going out with targets on our backs," Clint told him.

"I will be guided by your wisdom, Clint."

"Emrys," Clint said, "why don't you tell me something."

"Tell you what?"

"Anything," Clint said. "Tell me how you make things float through the air. Tell me how you managed to escape being shot. Or tell me about your name. Did you really choose it because it was Merlin's last name?"

"My friend," Emrys said, "there are truths I could tell you that you simply would not believe. What would that do to our friendship?"

"Friendships don't usually last, Emrys, when one friend is keeping secrets from the other."

"I understand how you feel, but . . ."

"Okay," Clint said, "okay, a friend also doesn't push another friend when he doesn't want to be pushed. Let me go back to the beginning. Tell me . . . something."

The waiter came with their steaks. They waited until he had served them and departed.

"Very well," Emrys said. "My name. It is indeed true that it was the last name of Merlin."

"So that's why you took it?"

"It is as good a name as any."

"Any chance you'll tell me your real name?"

"Well," Emrys said, "there is always a chance."

Morley had the Chinese whore on her back and was pounding her, driving his rigid cock into her as fast as he could. She was making groaning and squeaking noises, and he was building up a sweat until he finally exploded with a wild yell. It felt as if her insides were grabbing him and milking him. When she had taken every drop from him, he fell over onto his back and stared at the ceiling.

"Shitfire, gal," he said. "You near to killed me."

She giggled, rubbed her small hand over his sweaty chest.

"You needed that," she said. "First the relaxing, and then the fucking."

He looked at her and said, "You got a mouth on you."

"You no like dirty talk?"

"I like it fine."

"You stay longer with Ling," she said, "and you see what else Ling can do with mouth."

"Good God," he said. He looked down at himself, saw that he was getting hard again. "Talk dirty some more."

She giggled and said, "I talk dirty all night," she said, and grabbed ahold of his cock.

Clint and Emrys finished their suppers and headed back to the hotel.

"No one is watching us," Emrys said.

"Everybody is watching us."

"No, I mean no one who means us any harm."

"How can you tell?"

"I can feel it."

"Did you feel it when somebody was on the roof, getting ready to shoot at you?"

Emrys didn't answer.

"You did, didn't you?" Clint asked. "You had something under your robe, to protect you from the bullet. That's why you weren't hurt."

"You examined my robe."

"You've got more than one robe."

"Perhaps," Emrys said, "the man has decided to simply leave us alone."

"You think so?" Clint asked. "I don't."

"What, then? Where is he?"

"Probably getting his bearings," Clint said. "He thought he killed you, and then he hears you're still alive. He must be wondering what the heck is going on. Why should he be any different from the rest of us?"

"So what is next, then?"

"We leave tomorrow," Clint said. "Head for the next town on my list. Let's see if he continues to follow us. If he does, I'll double back and grab him."

"You have a list?"

"Yes," Clint said. "When we leave here, we're going to Sheridan. It's a big town—bigger than any of these. You'll be able to sell a hell of a lot of tickets. In fact, you might be able to do your show more than one day."

"I usually only stay in a town one night," Emrys said.

"Is that a hard-and-fast rule?" Clint asked. "You could make a lot of money in a place like Sheridan."

"Not a rule really," Emrys said. "It is just the way I have been doing things."

"Well," Clint said, "you can make up your mind once we arrive there."

"When shall we leave?"

"Early," Clint said. "We can have breakfast first thing and get on the road."

"Do we need to see anyone first? The sheriff? Or Mr. Wright?" Emrys asked.

"We don't need to check in with anyone before we leave," Clint said. "All the sheriff cares about is that we go. He doesn't want any more shooting in his town. I suspect Mr. Wright feels the same."

"This all suits me nicely," Emrys said. "I am just about finished with the town of Kirby."

"To tell you the truth," Clint said as they reached the hotel, "so am I."

The Chinese whore massaged Morley's cock until it was hard again. Then, while continuing to stroke it, she started to kiss his chest, his belly, moved down to his thighs, and finally, swooped in and took his cock in her mouth.

"Oh, geez," he said as she started to suck him. She had an incredibly educated mouth, and he was helpless to do anything but enjoy it. He reached down to hold her head in place, hoping she wouldn't stop . . . ever.

Ling knew she had the man in her power, which meant she'd be able to milk a bunch of money out of him. She had him so enthralled she thought she might even be able to get him to fall asleep after, and stay all night. And if he woke, before he could decide to leave, she'd start working on him again with her hands, and her mouth. Few men could resist her, especially when she used that broken English accent on them, and talked dirty.

Men loved that dirty talk, especially from a tiny little *Chinee* gal.

She felt him start to tense, leaned her forearms on his thighs to hold him there, continued to suck him while he exploded, making sure that he'd be totally spent, and exhausted, by the time they were finished.

TWENTY-NINE

Clint awoke the next morning with the first light streaming through his window. He washed and dressed, tossed his saddlebags over his shoulder, picked up his rifle, and left the room. When he got downstairs, Emrys was sitting there, waiting for him.

"I have checked out," he said.

"It'll take me a minute."

Clint also checked out, paid his bill, and then he and Emrys went into the dining room for breakfast.

Morley woke up in the Chinese whore's bed. She was lying beside him, snoring lightly. He frowned. He'd never intended to stay with her all night. This was going to cost him a lot of money.

She'd also kept him busy all night, so he hadn't had time to think his situation over.

"Damnit," he swore, sitting up.

"Hey, lover," the whore said. "You want nice morning wake-up?"

122   J. R. ROBERTS

"No," he said, getting to his feet. "Listen, I did not say I wanted to stay all night."

"You so relaxed—or worn out—you fall asleep," she said. "I no have heart to wake you."

"Well, I don't want to pay for the whole night," he said, hopping on one foot, pulling on a boot.

She folded her arms and frowned at him.

"You better pay up, buster," she said in perfect English, "or we have ways of getting the money from you."

He stopped hopping and stared at her.

"Hey, you talk good English!"

"Yeah," she said, "and my name ain't Ling. But you're still paying what you owe. We got bouncers here that are bigger than a mountain."

He stared at her, then said, "Goddamnit!" He'd been took, and took good. She was really good at this job. "Okay, damnit. How much is it?"

After breakfast, Clint and Emrys walked to the livery to collect the wagon and their horses. They hitched the mare up and then walked her and the wagon around to the front. There they settled their bill, and Emrys climbed up into his seat.

"How long will it take us to get to Sheridan?" he asked.

"At least two days," Clint said, mounting Eclipse. "Maybe during that time you might tell me something else about yourself? Or show me a thing or two?"

"Maybe," Emrys said, picking up his reins. "One never knows what might happen."

Morley paid his bill and got out of the whorehouse with only a few dollars to spare. He'd allowed the Chinese whore to distract him completely. Now he had to race over to the hotel to make sure Clint Adams and the magician were still there.

Taking a chance that he might meet up with them in the lobby, he entered and rushed to the front desk.

"Sorry, sir," the clerk told him, "but they have both checked out and left."

"Goddamnit!" Morley swore. "When?"

"This morning."

"Where'd they go?"

"I don't know that, sir."

"Damnit!"

He stormed out of the hotel and headed straight for the livery stable. Instead of following them now, he was going to have to track them.

As he saddled his horse feverishly, he thought about the magician. He knew that he'd put a bullet right in his heart, and the only way he could have survived was to be the Devil himself. There could be no further doubt.

He paid his bill, using the last of his money, walked his horse out, and mounted up.

This was now a hunt for the Devil, and he was charged with getting it done.

THIRTY

After half a day's travel, Clint was convinced that they were not being followed.

"Do you think he gave up?" Emrys asked.

"Either that," Clint said, "or he's lost."

"I would prefer that," Emrys said. "I do not wish to deal with him."

Clint looked at the magician.

"You sound like you're saying you don't want to have to kill him," he said.

"It is not for me to kill," Emrys said. "It is very difficult for me, and I only ever do it to survive. Killing is for warriors like you."

"I don't like it either."

"I did not mean to imply that you do," the magician said. "And I do not say it comes for naturally to you. It is just a larger part of your life than it is mine."

"I can't argue with that," Clint said.

"The mare is ready," Emrys said. "We may proceed."

                         *   *   *

The tracks being left by the Magic Man's wagon were easy
to pick up and follow. Morley decided to hang back and not
take a chance on being seen by Clint Adams, or felt by the
Devil.

Since the bullet he had fired had not killed the Devil,
he knew he needed to find another way to kill him. So he
decided that when they got to wherever they were going, Ed
Morley was going to go to church.

If anyone could tell him how to kill the Devil, it would
be a priest.

They camped for the night, and Clint deliberately did not
watch Emrys make the campfire. He took care of the horses
and came to the fire when it was already blazing. He prepared the coffee, and them made some bacon and beans for
them to eat.

"I am getting used to this coffee," Emrys said.

"You're just realizing how good it is."

"And this concoction . . . it is wonderful."

"It's bacon and beans," Clint said. "Haven't you ever had
it before?"

"I do not believe so."

"What were you eating before you met up with me?"

"I would hunt," Emrys said, "but mostly dried meats."

"We can hunt tomorrow," Clint said. "We should come
across some fresh meat somewhere along the way."

"That would be excellent," Emrys said. "I would enjoy
seeing you shoot. Are you very accurate?"

"I hit what I shoot at."

"You remind me of . . . somebody."

"Who?"

"Someone from . . . my life," Emrys said.

"But telling me exactly who that is would reveal too much of yourself to me?"

"I told you," Emrys said. "The truth would only make you think me mad."

"Well, what if I told you I already think you're mad," Clint offered.

Emrys laughed and said, "That would not surprise me."

"Can you do that fire thing again?" Clint asked. "I mean, springing it on you like this, when you can't set it up beforehand."

Emrys held his hand over the flames, but instead of dipping his hand in and lighting his fingers, the flames suddenly leaped up and did it. The tip of his index finger glowed and burst into flame—and then he blew it out.

"How does that not burn your finger?" Clint exclaimed. "Damn, how do you do that?"

"Magic," Emrys said.

"Real magic?" Clint said, shaking his head. Until he could disprove it, how could he call the man a liar?

"What is real magic?" Emrys asked.

"Well, I don't know," Clint said, "and obviously you're not going to tell me."

"Perhaps at some point, I will."

"So I'll just have to keep waiting."

"And keep making me concoctions like this to eat," Emrys said. "More, please."

Clint spooned out the rest of the bacon and beans for the magician and said, "Tomorrow I'll see if we can get a deer."

Ed Morley had left Kirby so fast he had not stocked up on supplies. He made a fire, but had nothing but beef jerky to eat. But he felt that these were the sacrifices he had to make to bring down the Devil.

Never a religious man before, Morley was suddenly very aware of God in his life. And God would help him, he was sure of that.

He just needed some assurance from a priest.

Clint decided to stand watch, and when he told Emrys he would be doing that, the magician said, "There's no need. We will be protected."

"How?"

"The same way my wagon is protected."

"By magic."

Emrys stared at him.

"Well, if you don't mind, I'll just stand watch anyway."

"Not all night," Emrys said. "If you are determined to do this, I will take a turn."

"Suit yourself," Clint said. "I'll wake you in four hours."

"I will sleep outside the wagon tonight," Emrys said.

"That's up to you."

Clint made himself a fresh pot of coffee and sat by the fire with his rifle while Emrys made a bed for himself underneath the wagon.

He still wondered how Emrys had been able to do that fire trick, but he forced himself not to look into the fire.

Emrys was perhaps the strangest person Clint had ever met, from his name to his mannerisms. He felt like a man from another time and another place.

He was sure that Emrys's mannerisms and attitude were the man's attempt to seem different. It helped with his whole act. But Clint couldn't help wondering who he was, what his real name was, and where he came from.

It would be odd if in a former life he had, indeed, been a drummer or a snake oil salesman. He certainly had the talent to sell himself. He could have been from the East, or that feeling Clint had that he was from another place could have meant he was from Europe somewhere—maybe Great Britain. Taking his name from Merlin might lend itself to that possibility.

Clint had never been this curious about another person in his life before. He thought that he might actually ride with the man until he found the answers he was looking for.

One thing was for sure, though. For someone who claimed to have real magic, he sure snored like a regular fellow.

THIRTY-ONE

By the second night, both Clint and Emrys were convinced that their tail was back.

"I smelled his fire," Clint said when they camped for the night. "This morning."

"I felt him," Emrys said. "What should we do?"

"Well," Clint said, "I could ride back and grab him, but how do I prove he took the shot at you?"

"So what do we do? Just allow him to follow us again?" Emrys asked.

"Yes."

"And then what?"

"Once we get to Sheridan, I think I'll be able to spot him, and keep an eye on him."

"And if he tries to kill you or me again?"

"Then we can have him arrested."

"Or kill him."

"I thought you didn't want to kill anyone."

"I was thinking more of you."

"Right now the only thing we're going to kill is this fire, so we can get back on the trail."

"Are you sure he won't try to kill us out here?"

"No, I'm not," Clint said. "But I'm willing to take the risk. If he thinks he missed you back in town, he's going to want to get closer next time."

"Like, perhaps, in the crowd in front of my wagon during a performance?"

"Yes, like that. But once we spot him, we'll be able to identify him."

"Once again," he said, "I must bow to you on this matter."

"Good," Clint said. "Douse the fire, and I'll get the horses ready."

"As you wish."

When they camped that night, Clint knew they'd make Sheridan by midday.

During the day he had been able to bring down a deer with a single shot, which had impressed Emrys.

"That in itself," the magician, said, "was a kind of magic."

Clint butchered the deer and they took a couple of haunches with them, leaving the rest for the coyotes—or anyone else who might find it.

Clint built a spit from branches and rotated the meat over the fire. He made some beans to go along with it. He sliced some meat off, put it on plates with the beans, and handed Emrys one.

"This is wonderful," Emrys said. "I don't think you would find better meat on the king's reserve—I mean, a king's reserve."

"A king?"

"I mean, a private reserve of some kind," Emrys said.

"I see."

They ate, cut more meat, and ate some more.

"So tell me, Emrys," Clint said, "have you known many kings where you come from?"

"That was simply a slight slip of the tongue," the other man said. "You know there is no royalty in this country."

"I know that," Clint said. "I was just thinking maybe you were from another country."

"Indeed? Which country would that be?"

"I don't know," Clint said. "England? Ireland?"

Emrys didn't answer. He bit into his meat.

Morley found the butchered deer.

He shooed some coyotes away from it, sliced off a hunk for himself, then left the rest to the coyotes, who quickly returned to their meal.

He built a fire, held the meat over the flame with a sturdy branch, wishing he had some coffee to wash it down with.

Clint Adams had to be the one who'd shot the deer. Just for a moment Morley wondered if he and the Devil had left the deer behind for him. Maybe it was a joke. He didn't mind the joke, though, because the meat—though gamy—was good.

Perhaps the Devil was laughing, but it was Morley who would have the last laugh.

Emrys was on the second watch, but Clint couldn't sleep, so he rolled out of his bedroll and approached the fire.

"Can't you sleep?" Emrys asked.

"No," Clint said. "I need some more coffee."

He sat across the fire from Emrys and poured himself a cup.

"Why don't you get some more sleep?" Clint suggested.

"I need very little," Emrys said. "Often I simply lie awake, staring at the stars."

"Is that because you miss home?"

Emrys smiled.

"Why do I get the impression you are trying to pry something out of me about my history, Clint?"

"Well," Clint said, "you can't blame a guy for trying, can you?"

"No," Emrys said, "actually, you cannot."

They sat in silence for a while, and then Emrys said, "All right."

"All right . . . what?"

"I have decided to tell you something." He held up one finger. "One thing."

"Do I get to pick what it is?"

"No!"

"Fine. Go ahead."

"I am not from your country."

"What a shock," Clint said. "What country are you from?"

"I said one thing," Emrys said. "Perhaps, tomorrow, I will tell you one more."

"At that rate," Clint said, "I should have your whole history in about ten years."

THIRTY-TWO

When they drove into Sheridan, Emrys was impressed.

"This is a very . . . fruitful town," he said. "I can feel it. I think perhaps I will perform here for more than one day."

"Good," Clint said. "And I'm sure they have a mayor we can check in with. Let's go to the livery first."

The livery was large enough to house not only the horses, but the wagon as well.

"You some kinda showman?" the holster asked.

"That's right," Emrys said. "Some kind of showman."

"What's in the wagon?"

"My show," the magician said. "It would not be wise for you to try to enter the wagon. Do you understand?"

The man, obviously an employee and not the owner, said, "Well, sure."

"Take good care of these horses," Clint said.

"I will." The man, in his thirties and as homely as sin, spit some tobacco juice into the dirt and took the horses to their stalls.

"Hotel now?" Emrys asked.

"Right."

He smiled.

"I think I am getting the hang of this."

They got a room each, and then Clint took Emrys for a walk around town. He'd been there before, but not for a while. Sheridan had grown by leaps and bounds, and two strangers walking down the street was not as odd as it might have been in a smaller town.

"There is City Hall," Emrys said, pointing across the street.

"And there's a steak house right next to it," Clint said.

"Which one shall we go to first?" Emrys asked.

At that point both their stomachs growled and they headed for the steak house.

After they'd finished an excellent meal, it was still early enough to catch the mayor in his office. They entered the building, went to the second floor, found the mayor's office, and presented themselves to his assistant.

"And what kind of show is this?" the lovely young woman asked. She wore glasses, and a gray suit that could not hide her curves. She had auburn hair and pretty blue eyes.

"A magic show," Clint said.

She looked at Clint.

"You are a magician?" she asked.

"No," Clint said, "my friend is the magician."

She looked at Emrys, his derby hat, then looked back at Clint.

"You'll need a permit to perform."

"That's why we're here to see the mayor."

"The mayor doesn't give out the permits," she said.

"Then who does?" Clint asked.

"The permit office."

"And where is that?" Clint asked.

"Downstairs."

"Thank you."

He and Emrys turned to leave the room.

"There's a fee," she called out.

Clint looked at her over his shoulder.

"I think we'll be able to handle it."

They went downstairs and found the permit office. The clerk, a young man in his twenties, had them fill out the form, then he stamped it.

"And the permit?" Clint asked.

"Oh, I can't give you that until you have a location."

"And where would you suggest?" Clint asked.

"There are lots of areas in town good for putting on a show," the clerk said. "Uh, depending on how big your show is."

"Okay," Clint said, "we'll take a walk around town, find a location, and come back."

"It's almost five," the clerk said. "I have to close at five."

"Then we'll come back first thing in the morning," Clint said. "What time?"

"I get in at eight."

"We'll see you then."

"Um," the clerk said as they started to leave.

"Yes?" Clint asked.

"Which one of you is the magician?"

Clint pointed to Emrys and said, "He is."

Out on the street, Emrys said, "That was exhausting."

"Yes, it was," Clint said, "but I guess that's the way things are done in big towns."

"Shall we look for a site, then?" Emrys asked.

"Yes," Clint said. "And along the way maybe we should stop in at the sheriff's office."

"To tell him about the other man?"

"To tell him about me," Clint said. "I just like to check in with the law in towns like this, let them now I'll be around for a while."

"That's what comes from being a legend, then?"

"That's what comes from having a reputation," Clint said. "The kind that makes people want to shoot at you."

"That must be very difficult for you."

"Well," Clint said as they walked, "usually it's somebody looking for a reputation, but lately . . ."

"Lately it has become more . . . personal?"

Clint looked at him.

"How do you know that?"

"Logic," Emrys said.

"Not magic?"

"Maybe," the Magic Man said, "just a good guess."

THIRTY-THREE

Ed Morley rode into Sheridan slowly, his eyes taking in both sides of the street. He was looking for Clint Adams or the Devil, but when he saw the church at the end of one of the side streets, he changed direction.

He reined in his horse in front of the church and dismounted. It was a Catholic church, which didn't matter to him one way or the other.

He went up the steps and entered. The inside was cavernous, with stained glass windows and a lot of statues. There were a few women in the pews, praying. He walked to the front of the church and stood in front of the altar.

"Can I help you, my son?"

He turned quickly, saw a man in black, with a white collar. He also had white hair, but an unlined face.

"Are you the priest?"

"I am," the man said. "Father Nathan."

"Father," Morley said, "I need to talk to somebody about the Devil. Do you know about the Devil?"

"Yes, I do," the priest said. "I am very well acquainted with the Devil and his works."

"Do you believe the Devil walks on earth?"

"I believe he has," Father Nathan said. "I also believe the Devil has disciples who walk the earth."

"Disciples," Morley said.

"Yes."

"Yes," Morley said, "disciples!"

"Son," Father Nathan said, "do you want to sit down and talk?"

Morley looked at the priest and said, "Yes, yes, I want to sit down and talk."

"Then come this way . . ."

Clint and Emrys found the sheriff's office before they found a site for the show.

"Just let me do the talking," Clint said.

"Of course."

They went inside. There were three men there, all wearing badges. One was middle-aged, sitting behind a desk. The other two were younger, in their thirties, and were being dressed down in no uncertain terms.

"Do you both read me?" the sheriff demanded.

"Yessir," they said.

The sheriff looked past his deputies at Clint and Emrys, then said to his men, "That's all. Get out."

Both men left with their heads bowed.

"Good help hard to find?" Clint said.

The sheriff didn't respond. Instead he asked, "What can I do for you?"

"My name is Clint Adams," Clint said. "Just arrived in town."

The man stared at him, then asked, "What's the Gunsmith want in Sheridan?"

"Passing through," Clint said.

"And who's this?"

"My friend," Clint said. "He's a magician, and he'll be putting on some shows."

"You'll need a permit."

"Already filed for one. We just need to find a location."

"I thought you said you were passing through?"

"We are," Clint said, "but he's going to put on a few shows as we pass."

"What are you doin' here, then?"

"Just checking in," Clint said, "letting you know I'm in town."

"Are you looking for trouble?"

"No."

"Expecting trouble?"

"I never go looking, Sheriff, but I'd be foolish not to expect it."

"I guess so," the man said. "Well, my name is Baker. If you shoot anybody, you're gonna have to answer to me."

"I understand."

"Fine, then," Baker said. "Enjoy your stay."

As they started for the door, the lawman asked, "What hotel are you in?"

"A place called the Colonial."

"Okay," the lawman said. "If I need you, I know where to find you."

"Have a good day," Clint said.

Outside, in front of the office, Emrys said, "Do you think you should have told him about our friend?"

"No," Clint said, "no point in giving him a reason to ask us to leave already. Let's wait and see what happens."

"Then I suggest we keep looking for a site for our show."

"Our show?"

"Well . . . we did apply for the permit together."

"Okay," Clint said, "our show."

They started off down the street.

"How do you kill the Devil?" Morley asked the priest.

"By living a life that is pure," the priest said. "If we do not sin, we need not fear the Devil."

"What about the Devil on earth? His disciples?"

"Well, if a man is doing the work of the Devil," Father Nathan said, "then he can be killed like any other man."

"With a bullet?"

"Of course."

"No," Morley said, shaking his head, "I tried that already."

"What?"

"I said I tried that already. I shot him. He didn't die."

"My God," the priest said, "y-you shot someone? Who?"

"Well, I thought he was the Devil, but like you said, he must be a disciple of the Devil."

"W-Where did this happen?" the priest asked. "Where did you shoot him?"

"In the chest," Morley said, "but he didn't die. And I ain't tellin' you where."

"It wasn't here, in Sheridan?"

"No," Morley said, "of course not. I just got here."

Father Nathan looked around the church. The women who had been praying had left a few minutes ago. He and Morley were alone. He suddenly realized he could be in mortal danger.

But he should have been more concerned with this poor man's soul than with his own life.

"My son," the priest said, "would you like to make your confession?"

"What? A confession?" Morley asked, shaking his head. "I ain't Catholic, Father."

"No matter," Father Nathan said. "God can be forgiving to non-Catholics."

Morley looked closely at the priest, and came to a decision. He slid his gun from his holster.

"Would he forgive me for killing a priest?"

"Wha—"

Morley pulled the trigger.

THIRTY-FOUR

Morley left the priest lying on the pew, and walked out of the church. In front he looked around, didn't see anybody.

He had to kill the priest. While he hadn't made a confession in the Catholic sense, he had told him about shooting the Devil's disciple. He couldn't let him live after that.

He mounted up and rode back to the main street to find a livery, and a hotel.

The little boy came out of hiding after Morley rode away. He had heard the shot and immediately hid. Now he went into the church and looked around. He didn't see anyone.

"Father!"

No answer.

"Father Nathan?"

Still no answer.

He started down the center aisle toward the altar. He was an altar boy. He was going to look for Father Nathan in the sacristy, but when he reached one of the pews, he saw him, and saw the blood.

"Father?"

When the priest did not answer, the boy turned and ran from the church.

Sheriff Baker looked up from his desk when the door opened, saw the small boy of about eight run in. He stood there, breathing hard, sweating.

"What is it, son?" Baker asked.

"Father Nathan."

"What about him?"

"Somebody shot him."

"What?"

"He's dead, Sheriff," the boy said. "You better come quick."

"Goddamnit!" Baker said, grabbing his hat. "Show me!"

The sheriff made the boy stay outside the church and went inside. He walked down the center aisle, found the priest where the boy said he'd be. He moved into the aisle, leaned over the body, and checked it. He was dead, shot once.

The sheriff went back outside.

"What's your name, boy?"

"Kevin."

"Kevin, how many shots did you hear?"

"One."

"Did you see the man who fired it?"

"Not exactly."

"What do you mean, not exactly?"

"I saw a man come out of the church after the shot," Kevin said.

"What did he do?"

"Looked around, then got on his horse, and rode away."

"Which direction?"

Kevin pointed.

"And you didn't know this man?" Baker asked. "Had never seen him before?"

"No, sir, he was a stranger."

Stranger. Morley knew of only two strangers in town.

Clint and Emrys found an empty lot that had already been cleaned out. It was a perfect place to set up for a show, just off of the main street.

It was dusk, and they had been just about ready to quit when they found it.

"Okay," Clint said, "let's get the names of these streets so we can tell the clerk in the morning."

Sheridan's main street was actually called Main Street, and the cross street was Dakota.

"Okay," Clint said, "now I could use a drink."

"I saw a saloon around the corner."

They walked to the White Mule Saloon, went inside, and ordered two beers.

That's where they were when the sheriff came in with his deputies.

THIRTY-FIVE

Clint turned as the three lawmen came crashing through the batwing doors, their guns out.

"What the—" Clint said.

"Just take it easy, Adams," Baker said. "I told you if anyone died in town while you were here, I'd come and find you."

"Who died?" Clint asked.

"Father Nathan."

"A priest?"

"That's right," Baker said. "A Catholic priest."

"And you think I did it?"

"A stranger did it," Baker said, "and you two are the only strangers I know of in town. Now I have a witness, so he's gonna take a look at you."

"Well, trot him on in, then," Clint said.

"He's a small boy," Baker said. "I'm not bringin' him into a saloon. We're goin' to my office. Boys, take their guns."

"I don't have a gun," Emrys said, spreading his hands.

"And I'm not giving mine up," Clint said.

"Yeah, you are," Baker said, "or I'll plug you."

"You'll try," Clint said, "but I'll get you first."

The sheriff wet his lips.

"Sheriff?" one of the deputies said.

"I'll go with you so the witness can look at us," Clint said, "and I'll go willingly, not at gunpoint. And I won't give up my gun. Now how this goes is up to you."

The two deputies were nervous, waiting for word from their boss.

"All right," Baker said, "all right." He lowered his gun. "Put your guns away, boys."

The deputies holstered their guns, looking relieved.

The sheriff holstered his.

"Thank you," Clint said. "Okay, lead the way, Sheriff."

They walked to the jailhouse with the sheriff in the lead and the deputies bringing up the rear.

"When was the priest killed?" Clint asked.

"This afternoon."

"We've been walking around town all morning, looking for a site for our show," Clint said. "I'm sure a lot of people have seen us."

"What did you find?"

"A lot on the corner of Main and Dakota."

"I know it," the sheriff said. "It's been for sale for a while."

"Good," Clint said, "then it'll be available."

They got to the sheriff's office and went inside. A small boy was sitting in a chair, where the sheriff had told him to stay and not move.

"Okay, Kevin," he said, "look at these two men. Have you ever seen them before?"

Kevin took a good look at the two men, and shook his head.

"No, sir."

"Are you sure? You didn't see one of these men at the church after Father Nathan was shot?"

"No, sir."

"Okay, son," Baker said. "Go on home to your mother."

"Wait," Emrys said as Kevin got to his feet. The boy froze. Emrys reached out and seemingly plucked a two-bit piece from the boy's ear. "Here you go." He handed it to him.

"Wow! Thanks."

He felt his other ear, but decided to be happy with what he got and ran out.

Baker walked around and sat at his desk.

"I'm sorry," he said. "I didn't know what else to do."

"Well," Clint said, "maybe we can help."

"How?"

"We might know of another stranger."

"Who?"

Clint looked over at the potbellied stove.

"Is there any coffee in that pot?"

"Sure."

"Well, let's have some and I'll tell you."

Over coffee, Clint told Baker and his deputies about what had happened in Ten Sleep.

"So you think this fella might have followed you here?" the lawman asked.

"Could be."

"Why would he kill the priest?"

"I don't know," Clint said, "but I'm sorry to hear it."

Baker looked at his deputies.

"You boys get over to the undertaker's. Father Nathan's body has to be picked up from the church.

"Yes, sir."

As they left, Clint asked, "Is there another priest at the church?"

"Father Damon," Baker said. "He's in his seventies, mostly retired."

"Well," Clint said, "maybe he'll have to come out of retirement for a while."

"I'll talk to him. You can't tell me what this stranger looks like who took a shot at you?"

"We've never seen him," Clint said. "We were hoping that if he followed us here, we'd spot him."

"Why didn't you just track him down out there and kill him?" Baker asked.

"Because," Clint said, "that's the kind of thing I could be arrested for."

"Yeah," Baker said sourly, "you're right."

"We've worked up an appetite walking around town," Clint said. "You mind if we go and get something to eat?"

"No, go ahead," Baker said. "Try the Magnolia Café. Best steaks in town."

"We ate at the steak house next to City Hall."

"Not good. Go to the Magnolia."

"Okay, thanks, Sheriff. And thanks for not plugging me."

"Thanks for not shootin' me," Baker said.

They left the office.

THIRTY-SIX

After leaving the church, Ed Morley found a livery and a hotel that were both small and run-down. He left his horse, got himself a room, then began to walk around town, watching carefully for Clint Adams and the Devil.

He was across the street from the White Mule Saloon when they came walking out with three lawmen. He ducked into a doorway and watched Clint Adams and the Devil being walked to the jailhouse. But Adams still had his gun, so he didn't think they were under arrest.

Once they had all gone into the jail, he found a new position across the street, and watched.

At the Magnolia, more a full-service restaurant than a café, they got a table in the rear of a large service floor and ordered two steak dinners. When they came, the steaks were perfectly cooked, as were the vegetables.

"Better than my bacon and beans, eh?" Clint asked.

"I like the bacon and beans," Emrys said, "but this is very good."

Clint told the waiter he wanted strong coffee, and he got it.

"Do you think our friend killed the priest?" Emrys asked.

"It's a large town," Clint said. "There could be a killer here somewhere that has nothing to do with us—but that would be a hell of a coincidence."

"But why would he kill the priest?"

"The priest might have seen something," Clint said, "or maybe our man said something he shouldn't have. If it's a Catholic church, maybe he made a confession and then immediately regretted it."

Emrys frowned.

"What is it?"

"If we brought that man here, then we are to blame for the priest's death."

"That's stretching the blame, Emrys," Clint said. "The blame belongs to the man who pulled the trigger."

"Yes," Emrys said, "all right."

Morley was across the street from the Magnolia, once again watching. He wanted to find out what hotel the two men—or the man and the Devil's disciple—were staying in. Then he could decide his next move.

He had located the disciple. Talking to the priest had paid off. Killing him had been necessary, but now he knew he wasn't dealing with the actual Devil.

He was dealing with something he could kill.

Emrys suddenly sat up straight in his chair. He looked as if he had been struck by lightning.

"What is it?" Clint asked.

"He's here."

"Where?"

"I don't know," Emrys said, looking around. "I can just . . . feel him."

Clint didn't consider that to be magic, since he had his own instincts.

"Inside?" Clint asked. He looked around at the other tables. "One of these diners?"

"No, I do not think so."

"Outside, then."

"Perhaps."

Clint looked at the window, but didn't get up and walk to it. Standing in front of a plate glass window was not healthy.

"Okay," he said, "if he's out there, he'll do one of two things when we leave."

"Shoot at us," Emrys said.

Clint nodded.

"Or follow us to see where we're staying."

"And what will we do?"

"If he wants to follow us," Clint said, "we'll let him."

"And if he wants to shoot us?"

Clint looked at the magician.

"Then I'll shoot back."

THIRTY-SEVEN

At the last minute, Morley decided to stay in the shadows and not move. Darkness had already fallen. The Devil's disciple might feel him there.

When they left the Magnolia Café, he followed them, but only with his eyes. They walked down Main Street. He craned his neck to keep them in sight as they walked in and out of the circles of light thrown by the streetlamps.

Finally, he saw them stop and go into a hotel. He waited a long time before leaving his hiding place.

"He did not follow us," Emrys said in the hotel lobby.

"I didn't feel him either."

"Oh, I felt him," Emrys said, "watching. But he did not follow."

"Well, if he watched us, then he can figure out where we're staying."

"So what now?"

"I'll take a look from my window," Clint said. "Meanwhile—"

"Stay away from my window," Emrys said. "Yes, I know."

"If he's out there," Clint said, "I'll go out the back and see if I can sneak up on him and say hello."

"At which time you will let me know, yes?"

"Yes," Clint said, "I will."

They went up to the second floor and split up in the hall.

Emrys went up to his room, sat on the bed, calmed himself, and closed his eyes. In his head he saw Clint Adams in his room, moving toward the window . . .

Clint stood to the side and peered out his window, which overlooked Main Street. It was dark, and while the street was lined with streetlamps, they threw as many shadows as they did circles of light.

He watched for a good half hour. If there was a man across the street, he was very good at staying still. Clint did not even see the glowing tip of a cigarette, which might have been a giveaway.

He continued to watch . . .

Morley felt powerful.

He felt as if his body had been invaded by another spirit, one who kept him calm, collected . . . and invisible.

What if his battle with the Devil and his disciple—had become known in Heaven, and an Angel had been sent to earth to bond with him, and help him in his fight?

He felt as if he could see and smell *everything* so clearly!

If the disciple could work for the Devil, then why couldn't Ed Morley work for God?

Emrys knew the man was there, but there was something different about him. It did not feel as if he was a normal man. Something had changed. Something he should probably have warned Clint about, but if he did, then his friend would surely think he was mad . . .

Clint wondered if the man was gone.

How could anyone stay still for so long? Even if he was in the dark across the street, his instincts could usually pick up some kind of movement.

Where the hell was he?

But Morley had never believed in God.

Neither had he ever thought much about the Devil, until recently.

He wanted a cigarette, but didn't dare light one. It would be a dead giveaway to his position, if anyone was watching.

He was in the doorway of a store that had closed hours earlier. He'd been standing for some time and where, in the past, he may have had to flex his legs to keep them from cramping, he was fine now. He could have stood this way for hours more.

He just didn't feel like the same man. Certainly the same man who had shot the priest, but not the same man who had left Ten Sleep.

Clint decided to go out and see what he could find.

He left his room, went down the stairs. In the lobby the clerk was dozing, his head down on the desk. Clint sneaked past him and took a back hallway to the rear of the hotel. He found the back door, and went out.

He was in a darkened alley, stood still for a while until his eyes had adjusted to the dark. When he could see, he worked his way along to a side alley, and then to the mouth of it.

Main Street was quiet, nobody walking back and forth. He could hear sounds from the saloon down the street. He slid from the alley, moved away from the hotel for half a block, then crossed over to the other side. From there he began to work his way back in the direction of the hotel until he was near the doorway right across from it. He still could not see anyone.

He made his final move, which was to move quickly to the doorway, trying to catch the watcher by surprise.

Three darkened doorways of three closed stores, and they were all empty.

Nobody was there?

Nobody had ever been there?

Or somebody *had* been there, but was gone now?

It was amazing.

Morley instinctively knew that someone was coming for him. He was able to leave his hiding place and move farther down the street, toward the saloon. From there he watched and waited, finally saw a shadow moving toward his former hiding place.

The Gunsmith?

He was so tempted to just step out into a nearby circle of light and try him, but he was only the secondary target. The magician—the Devil's disciple—he was the main target.

So he remained where he was and watched . . .

Disappointed—and more confused than he'd been in some time—Clint crossed to the hotel and went back inside. The clerk was still asleep with his head on the desk. Clint went up to the second floor and knocked on Emrys's door.

"He was gone," Clint said, "or he was never there."

"He was there," Emrys said. "Come in."

"We need to turn in," Clint said, "get an early start tomorrow to obtain that permit."

"Come in," Emrys said again. "There are some things I should tell you."

THIRTY-EIGHT

Clint entered the room, wondering if the magician was finally going to truly tell him something about himself.

But he never could have guessed what it would be.

"I do not think the man who is watching us and following us is a man."

"What? If he's not a man, then what is he, Emrys? And for that matter, what are you?"

"I am a man," Emrys said. "Perhaps not from here, and perhaps not a man like any other you have ever met, but a man nevertheless."

"Okay," Clint said, "that's damned unclear. So what is he?"

"He may have started out as a man, but I believe he has become obsessed."

"Obsessed?" Clint asked. "With what? You?"

"Not with what," Emrys said, "by what?"

"Emrys," Clint said, "you're making no sense to me at all."

"I am just trying to say that you should be careful with

this man," Emrys said. "I know that you have never found anyone faster than yourself with a gun, but this man . . . he is not normal."

"He's not normal," Clint said. "You are a man unlike any other man, but still a man. Hey, I got it."

"Did you find him out there?"

"I didn't."

"And yet he was there. What does that tell you?"

"That I'm getting old."

"And if you want to get any older," Emrys said, "you will heed my warnings."

"We better turn in," Clint said. "We've got to get you set up for your show tomorrow."

Clint left Emrys's room, convinced that the magician was never going to speak plainly to him.

In fact, he was probably incapable of that.

After Clint left his room, Emrys wondered if he should have spoken more plainly to the man. Would he have been able to understand and, more important, accept?

Probably not. It was probably better to leave it the way it stood.

Morley decided the deed needed to be done the next day. He would turn in for the night, and wake up ready and willing to do what he had to do to slay the Devil's disciple.

He turned and walked away from the hotel, into the dark.

In the morning, Clint and Emrys fetched the wagon from the livery, hooked it up to the mare, and took it over to the lot. While they were setting up, Sheriff Baker came walking by.

"The word's gotten out already," he said to them. "You're gonna have a crowd."

"We have not even sold any tickets yet," Emrys said.

"Well then, you better get out there before the folks start showin' up."

Neither Clint nor Baker saw where Emrys had gotten the handful of tickets he was holding out to Clint. One moment his hand was empty, and the next moment they were there.

Clint took the tickets, shaking his head.

"That was amazing," Baker said.

"He's just a big show-off."

"Come on," Baker said, "I'll show you the best places to get rid of those tickets."

With the sheriff's guidance, Clint was able to get rid of all the tickets in just over an hour. The performance was scheduled for three, which gave them a little over two hours to finish setting up.

Baker walked Clint back to the site to see that some people had already begun to gather.

"I'll move them back," he said. "If they stand around waitin' too long, there's bound to be some trouble."

"Appreciate that, Sheriff."

As the sheriff walked away, Clint approached the wagon, which was closed up tight. Emrys was nowhere to be seen, so he was obviously inside.

"Emrys!" Clint called out.

When there was no answer, he knocked on the doors of the wagon, then heard the footsteps from inside. He was determined not to let the echoing sound of those steps play on his mind.

The doors opened and Emrys appeared.

"The tickets are sold," Clint told him.

"Very good," the magician said. "You have done your part, so now I must do mine."

"Is there anything else you want me to do?" Clint asked.

"No," Emrys said, "unless you can make sure to keep us alive."

"That will be my priority."

"Excellent."

Emrys went back into the wagon, closing the doors behind him. Moments later the side of the wagon came down to form a stage.

The people who were milling about began to clap their hands in anticipation. The sheriff finally stepped aside and just allowed the crowd to close around the wagon.

Morley moved in among the crowd, having changed from his trail clothes into some newer duds he'd bought from the mercantile. He was wearing a jacket, and also had a new gun and shoulder holster beneath it. Some of the money he had used to purchase these items had come from the poor box at the church. After he'd killed the priest, he robbed the box. There wasn't much there, but it had been enough.

He took up position in the center of the crowd, his arm folded across his chest, waiting for the show to begin.

THIRTY-NINE

Clint stood stage right. From there he could watch Emrys, and the crowd as well. Emrys mesmerized his audience with feats of magic like levitation, making items disappear and reappear, and causing items to appear in people's pockets. Clint was watching very closely, but could not see how the man was doing it.

But he was also watching the crowd, alert for anyone with a gun, so he might have missed something. He must have missed something, for there was no way Emrys could be doing those things without some sort of trick.

Morley watched the performance and, despite himself, was amazed. The things that the magician was doing convinced him that he truly was dealing with a disciple of the Devil. There was no other way he could be making those things happen. He made a gun disappear, he made it float, and he made playing cards appear in the pockets of people in the crowd. Unless those people were working with him—but how could they be? The magician was a stranger in this town. Just like Morley was.

The Devil's work.

By the time Emrys came to the end of his act, no one had stepped forward with a gun and tried to kill him. Maybe, Clint thought, the next performance.

After the sheriff had dispersed the crowd, Clint once again knocked on the back doors of the wagon.

"Folks are gone," he said when Emrys opened the doors. "You want to get something to eat?"

"Yes," Emrys said, "I am very hungry."

He stepped down, having removed his robe and left it behind.

"He did not make an attempt this time," the magician said as they walked. "Perhaps later this afternoon."

"That's what I'm afraid of," Clint said.

They walked to town, stopped in a café to eat, where people waved to them, recognizing them from the performance.

"I now find performing in this town questionable," Emrys said. "I do not like being recognized wherever I go."

"Then you might try leaving that derby hat in your wagon in the future."

Emrys frowned, touched his hat, then removed it and put it on a nearby chair.

They ordered steaks, Emrys having decided it was all he liked to eat when they weren't on the trail.

They were halfway through their meal when Sheriff Baker appeared in the doorway. He spotted them and crossed the room to join them.

"Have a seat, Sheriff," Clint invited him.

"Don't mind if I do." The lawman sat down and looked at Emrys. "That was some show you put on."

"Thank you."

"Those were really some amazing tricks."

Emrys didn't respond.

"He doesn't like them to be called tricks," Clint said.

"Oh," Baker said, "Sorry. What should I call them?"

"He just likes it to be called . . . magic."

"Oh," Baker said, "okay, magic. It was amazing magic." Baker leaned close to Clint. "How does he make things float like that?"

"I have no idea," Clint said.

"Have you made any progress in finding out who killed the priest?" Emrys asked, changing the subject.

"I haven't," Baker said. "All I know is whoever did it also robbed the poor box."

"Is it a wealthy church?" Emrys asked.

"Not at all," Baker said. "It's very poor. The old priest said there was hardly any money in the box."

"That is too bad," Emrys said.

"Guess your man either wasn't there for the show, or decided not to make a try this time," Baker said.

"I'll be watching the crowd this afternoon real close," Clint told him.

"Well, I'll be there, too, watching," Baker said. He leaned close to Clint again. "I wanna see if I can figure out how he does them tri—I mean, that magic."

Morley decided there was only one place you could kill a disciple of the Devil.

In church.

That meant that, somehow, he had to get the magician to the church. And if possible, alone.

* * *

The second show went off without a hitch. No sign of a gun in anyone's hand. Emrys's magic amazed and bewildered everyone, including Clint.

He couldn't watch too closely, though. Just in case there was a gun in the crowd. So he still didn't know how the magician did it. Maybe one day he'd find out, but not today.

Not today.

Morley went to the church. There were no parishioners praying this time. None working on the outside of the church. Seated in the front pew was a white-haired priest. As Morley approached, the man turned his heavily lined face to the younger man. He had blue eyes that were a startling contrast to his dry, leathery skin and white hair.

"Can I help you?"

"You the priest?"

"I am."

"What's your name?"

"Father Damon."

"Well, Father," Morley said, "I do need some help from you."

"That is why I'm here, my son," Father Damon said. He stood. He was old and brittle, but still tall. "What is it you need?"

"I need your help, Father," Morley said, "to kill the Devil's disciple."

Clint and Emrys moved the wagon back to the livery, and while Clint returned to the hotel, the magician climbed into the wagon and cleaned up after the show. He was inside when someone knocked on the doors.

Emrys opened them, saw a dirty little boy of about ten standing there.

"Can I help you, boy?"

The boy stared up at him in awe, his eyes wide. He was obviously frightened out of his wits.

"Come on, boy," Emrys said. "Speak up."

"Father Damon sent me."

"Father Damon?"

"Yessir. He's the onliest priest we got now that Father Nathan's dead."

"And what does Father Damon want with me?"

"It ain't him, sir," the boy said. "It's the other man. The one with the gun."

"A man with a gun? At the church?"

"Yessir."

"What does he want?"

"He wants you, mister."

"Me?"

"He told me to go and get the magician," the boy said. Then with a frown, he added, "An' he said somethin' about you bein' the Devil's de—desci—decible?"

"Disciple?" Emrys asked. "The Devil's disciple?"

"That's it!" the boy said excitedly. "He said, 'The Devil's disciple.'"

"Ah-ha," Emrys said. "I see."

"Will you be comin', mister?"

"Yes," Emrys said, "yes, I will be coming. But first you must do something for me."

The boy looked past Emrys, into the darkness of the wagon.

"Mister," he said, "you don't want me to go in . . . there, do you?"

"Eh?" Emrys said. Then he reached behind him and, to the boy's relief, closed the doors.

"No, no," the magician said, "no one goes in there. No, here is what I wish you to do . . ."

FORTY

Morley waited in front of the altar, his gun already in his hand. The elderly priest, Father Damon, was sitting in the front pew. Morley had instructed him to stay there and not move.

The boy entered the church, and Morley shouted, "Stop there!"

The boy stopped.

"Is he comin'?" Morley asked.

"He's comin', sir," the boy said. "He said he'd be right here."

"Okay," Morley said. "Come closer."

The boy started down the aisle. When he got halfway, Morley snapped, "Stop!"

The boy stopped short, hunching his shoulders.

"Here." Morley threw the boy two bits. The coin flipped through the air, and the boy caught it neatly in one hand.

"Good boy!" Morley said. "Now get out of here."

"What about Father Damon?"

"The priest stays!"

"But—"

"Get out!"

The boy turned and ran outside, where Emrys was waiting.

"He won't let Father Damon leave," the boy told the magician.

"That's all right," Emrys said. "Now go and do what I told you to do."

"Yes, sir."

The boy raced off, and Emrys turned toward the church doors.

The boy ran to the hotel and pounded on Clint's door.

Clint was inside, washing his face in the basin. He grabbed a towel and dried his hands on the way to the door, then answered it with his hand in his gun.

When he saw the boy, he said, "What can I do for you, son?"

"Mr. Adams," the boy said, "the magician sent me . . ."

As Emrys entered the church, he felt the ripples in the atmosphere. It told him what he had feared was true. The man with the gun was no longer just a man; he was a man on a mission.

The magician saw the priest sitting in the front pew, saw the man with the gun standing in front of the altar.

"Come on in," the man with the gun said. "My name is Morley."

"Your name is of no importance," Emrys said. "I know who you are."

"Is that a fact?"

"Yes."

"Well, no matter, then," Morley said. "We both know what I'm here to do."

"We know what you are here to try to do."

"I have to destroy you," Morley said. "That is my mission."

"You do not know what you are doing, Morley," Emrys said. "This is not even you."

"It doesn't matter who I am," Morley said. "It only matters what I am here to do."

"And you are going to do it with that gun?"

"This gun?" Morley waved it. "This isn't the gun I shot you with before, but it will do."

"It will not kill me," Emrys said. "You know that. You have already seen that."

"It may not kill you," Morley said, pointing the gun at Father Damon, "but it will kill the priest."

The priest had not moved since Emrys entered the church.

"If he is even still alive," Emrys said.

Morley, still pointing the gun at the priest, said, "Stand up, Father Damon."

The priest stood.

"Tell the magician you are alive."

Father Damon turned to face Emrys. His lined face was sad, his eyes pained.

"I am . . . alive," he said to Emrys, "if you can call this existence a life."

"Sit down and shut up," Morley said.

The priest sat down.

"If I shoot this priest, I would be putting him out of his misery."

"I can see that."

"You should have killed me," Father Damon said, "not Father Nathan. He was a good man."

"And you are not?" Emrys asked.

"I have lived my life," Father Damon said. "Father Nathan's life was ahead of him. I am . . . finished."

"Never mind this," Morley said. "The priest—neither of them—is the reason we are here. You are."

"On the contrary," Emrys said. "I think the reason we are here is you."

"You, me," Morley said with a shrug. "It is all the same."

Emrys moved his hands, and Morley cocked the hammer of his gun, pointed it at the priest again.

"No magic, magician!" he snapped.

Emrys stopped.

"If you somehow produce a gun, I'll kill the priest before I kill you."

"Once you kill the priest," Emrys said, "you have no hold on me. No way to stop me."

"But I do have the priest," Morley said. "I want you to walk to me with your hands held away from your body."

"Very well."

Emrys spread his arms, and began walking down the aisle toward the man with the gun.

At that point Clint Adams entered the church and saw what was going on.

"Hold it right there!" he said.

FORTY-ONE

"I don't know what's going on here," Clint said, "but it stops now."

Emrys stopped halfway down the aisle.

Morley leaned over to look past the magician at Clint.

"Adams," Morley said. "Nice of you to join us. You might notice I have my gun pointed at this priest."

"I did notice that."

"Then if I was you, I'd take my gun out and drop it to the floor."

Clint hesitated. He rarely, if ever, gave up his gun if he could help it. He wondered if he could draw and fire around Emrys and hit Morley before he could shoot the priest. If it had been only his life he was playing with, he would have tried it.

"I know what you're thinkin'," Morley said, "and you'll never make it. My finger is already on the trigger."

"Shoot him," the priest called out. "Don't worry about me. I don't matter."

"Shut up!" Morley told the priest. "Come on, Adams, make up your mind."

Damnit. He was going to have to depend on Emrys having some trick up his sleeve. The magician was not wearing his robe, just jeans and a shirt. Clint couldn't see anywhere he might have a gun hidden on him, but he'd seen the man produce things out of thin air before.

"Well?"

Clint removed his gun from his holster with two fingers and dropped it to the floor.

"Very good," Morley said. "If all I wanted to do was kill you, Adams, I'd shoot you now where you stand, but you're not my number one target."

"Why'd you kill the other priest?" Clint asked.

"It was necessary," Morley said. "After I finished talkin' to him, he knew why I was here."

"And why would you kill this older priest?" Emrys asked.

Morley shrugged and said, "Oh, because I can."

"Because you're evil, Morley," Emrys said.

"I'm evil?" Morley asked. "You are the one working for the Devil. I'm here doing God's work."

"God's work?" Clint asked. "Killing priests?"

"Killing disciples of the Devil!" Morley said.

"What the hell are you talking about?" Clint asked.

"How else can you explain the things he does?" Morley asked. "Makin' things float and disappear. That's the Devil's work."

"He's a magician, Morley," Clint said. "There are explanations for the things he does."

"Explanations for magic?" Morley asked.

"They're tricks," Clint said. "Tell him, Emrys."

"The Gunsmith thinks you do cheap tricks, magician. Or should I say, wizard?"

"You may call me whatever you like," Emrys said. He

still had his arms straight out from his sides, much like the figure on the crucifix behind Morley.

"Tell him, Emrys," Clint said. "Tell him how it is you do your tricks."

"He doesn't know, does he?" Morley asked Emrys. "The Gunsmith doesn't know the truth."

"What truth?" Clint asked. "What's he talking about?"

"I told you," Morley said. "He works for the Devil."

"Jesus," Clint said, "you're crazy, Morley. I should have tracked you on the trail and put you down days ago."

Morley laughed.

"You might have succeeded days ago," he said, "but not now."

"Why not now?" Clint asked.

"Because," Emrys said, "now he is more than just a man."

"And you're sounding crazy, too," Clint said. "The both of you. Why don't you just let me take the priest out of here and you two can settle things between you?"

"Now, now," Morley said, "I wouldn't want you and the priest to miss everything."

Clint wondered if he should make a grab for his gun off the floor. It might have been a mistake to drop it, after all.

"Okay," Morley said, "now that that's all settled, magician, you can just keep walkin' toward me—and keep your hands out."

FORTY-TWO

Emrys started moving forward again.

Clint wondered what the magician had in mind. He had come to the church alone. But he had also sent the young boy to fetch him. He must have had something he wanted Clint to do.

The priest sat stiffly and would be of no help at all. Clint had the distinct feeling that the man actually wanted to die.

As Emrys continued to move toward Morley, he was squarely between Clint and the gunman.

Morley kept his gun pointed at the priest as he watched Emrys approach.

Clint wondered if Morley's plan was simply to wait until Emrys was very close, and then shoot the magician at point-blank range. There was no way Emrys would be able to survive that.

He was waiting for Emrys to do . . . something!

"This is a big mistake, Morley," Emrys finally said.

"I hear you're callin' yourself Emrys," Morley said. "Does Adams know the meaning of that?"

"He knows it's my name," Emrys said. "That is all."

"But it's not your only name," Morley said.

"It does not matter."

"You mean you don't wish to be called Merlin?"

"No more than you wish to be called . . . Modred."

Merlin?

Modred?

What the hell were they talking about? Those were names from the stories of King Arthur. Were they both completely deranged, thinking they were characters from the Knights of the Round Table?

Clint decided to keep quiet and listen. At some point it might become time for him to snatch up his gun.

"I suppose the names we're using will do," Morley said. "Keep coming, Emrys."

Emrys had almost reached Morley. This was going to come to an end one way or another.

Suddenly, Clint became aware that someone was speaking. He listened, realized that it was the priest. He was praying.

Morley heard him, too, and frowned.

"Stop that!"

Father Damon kept on.

"I said stop that praying!" Morley snapped.

"You're going to kill him," Clint said. "Why not let him make peace with God?"

"I am God's instrument here!" Morley said. "If he wants to pray, he should pray to me."

"Well," Clint said, "you're a little full of yourself, aren't you?"

Father Damon's droning got louder. It was actually starting to bother Clint, too.

"That is close enough," Morley said to Emrys. He was

as close as he was going to get while still being beyond arm's reach.

Morley took the barrel of the gun from the priest and pointed it at Emrys's forehead.

"This will be a good test," Morley said. "I shot you once before and you survived."

"And if I survive again this time?"

"Then I will find another way to kill you."

"And how would that be?"

"I will use the priest."

"To kill me?"

"Priest," Morley said, "tell my friend what your specialty used to be when you were younger."

Father Damon licked his dry, cracked lips and said, "Exorcism."

"Exorcism?" Clint said. "What the hell—"

"That's enough!" Morley said. "First we will try it my way."

His finger tightened on the trigger. At that point Clint saw the fingers of Emrys's hands move. Just the fingers, in a "come here" motion.

From behind the altar, the six-foot crucifix suddenly leaped off the wall—it didn't fall off, it leaped.

Morley heard it and moved just in time to keep from being struck by it.

"Ha!" he said to Emrys, but by the time he realized his mistake, it was too late.

Clint dove down to the floor, came up with his gun, and fired.

FORTY-THREE

Sheriff Baker came out of the church, found Clint and Emrys standing by the wall.

"Okay," Baker said, "the priest supports your story. I have some men carrying the body out now."

He stepped aside. Two men came walking out, carrying Morley's body.

"Where's the priest?" Clint asked.

"Inside."

"How is he?"

"That's hard to say," Baker replied. "He hasn't moved."

"I want to talk to him," Emrys said.

"Sure," Baker said.

Emrys went inside.

"Was this the man—" Baker started.

"Yes," Clint said, "this was the man."

"Then it looks like your problems are solved."

"My problems are never solved, Sheriff," Clint said. "They're only postponed."

"Well . . . don't leave town until I tell you. Okay?"

"Okay," Clint said. He turned and went into the church. Emrys was sitting in the front pew with Father Damon. Emrys was leaning into the priest, who was still sitting motionless and erect.

Clint walked down the center aisle. When Emrys heard him, he leaned away from the priest.

"Father Damon, are you okay?" Clint asked.

"I am . . ." he said. But it didn't sound like he meant, "I am fine." It sounded like he was simply saying, "I am."

"What was all that business about exorcism?" Clint asked.

"That was many years ago, in Mexico," Father Damon said.

"Am I right about what exorcism means?" Clint asked.

"Cleansing people of the Devil's possession," Emrys said. "If that is what you think."

"That's it," Clint said. "So Morley thought you were possessed by the Devil?"

"Or Morley himself was possessed," Father Damon said.

"He was?" Clint asked. "Or he thought he was?"

Father Damon looked at Clint and asked, "What is the difference?"

The next day Clint and Emrys were eating lunch in another café in Sheridan. Clint had finally convinced Emrys to order something other than steak. They were both eating beef stew when Sheriff Baker walked in.

"I've spoken to the judge," the lawman said, sitting with them. "You fellas are free to go or stay, as you please."

"I pick go," Clint said.

"No more performances?" Baker asked.

"No," Emrys said. "It is time for me to leave, find . . . smaller venues."

"Smaller?" Baker asked.

"Yes," Emrys said. "Too much attention here."

"Ah," Baker said. "Well, can't say I'll be sorry to see the two of you go," The lawman stood up. "I don't need any more excitement in my town."

He touched his hat and left the café.

"If you don't want any more attention," Clint asked Emrys, "why would you continue to travel around, doing magic?"

"Because it is what I do," the magician said.

"So are you a magician, or a wizard, like Morley said?"

"What is the difference?"

"I don't know," Clint said. "He seemed to think there was one. Aren't they the same thing?"

"Basically."

"And what was that business with the names?" Clint asked. He had looked them up again in his copy of *Le Morte d'Arthur.* "Merlin? Modred?"

"You know where those names are from," Emrys said.

"From fiction," Clint said.

"Or history."

"Emrys . . . I can't ride with you anymore."

"I know."

"Unless you're ready to tell me more."

"I am afraid I can't do that," Emrys said. "I think you may have already seen too much."

"That is," Clint added, "if I can figure out what it is I saw."

Clint walked with Emrys to the livery stable. He was going to pick up Eclipse, while the magician claimed his wagon, and then they'd go their separate ways.

Clint saddled Eclipse and walked him out the back,

where Emrys had hitched his mare to the wagon. They both
walked to the front, leading their horses.

"I don't suppose there's a chance I can get a look inside
the wagon, is there?" Clint asked.

"You've seen the inside."

"I know," Clint said. "I just thought . . . another look."

"Of course."

Clint was surprised. Emrys walked to the rear of the
wagon and opened the doors. The sun lit up the interior and
Clint saw nothing that he hadn't seen before—sacks and
barrels of supplies, other items hanging on the sides that fit
into Emrys's act. The man's robe was hanging on a nail.
From what he could see, there was only one robe, so this
had to be the one he'd been wearing when Morley shot him
in the chest. Clint still could not explain why there was no
hole, no blood, no injury.

"Have you seen enough?" Emrys asked.

"I suppose so."

Emrys closed the doors.

"Where are you heading?" the magician asked.

"South," Clint said. "To Texas. What about you?"

"I am not sure," Emrys said. "I suppose I will just continue west."

The two men shook hands.

"You're the most unusual man I've ever met," Clint said.

"Perhaps we'll meet again in the future," Emrys said.

As the magician drove away in his wagon, Clint wondered how far into the future he might have been looking.

Watch for

THE SALT CITY SCRAPE

389th novel in the exciting GUNSMITH series
from Jove

Coming in May!

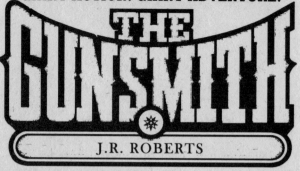

GIANT ACTION! GIANT ADVENTURE!

THE GUNSMITH

J.R. ROBERTS